The Devil Thinks I'm Pretty

Apocalypse Party
Design by Mike Corrao

Paperback:978-1-954899-66-7

The Devil Thinks I'm Pretty

Charlene Elsby

Part One

1

The devil thinks I'm pretty.

The devil thinks I'm smart.

The devil says that I choose for myself.

But that he's always for me.

He's always been there.

The devil's always been there for me.

I felt it when I did the things I've done.

I'm always of two minds about it, but both of them, I think, are wrong. Sometimes I think that if the devil were in me, he'd have done more right by me. Like you always think of the devil with respect to some tall businessman in a pinstripe suit and his hair slicked back. You don't know if the devil's there at all until he turns around, and you see his tail, just for a second, or maybe you didn't. You think that if you're in with the devil, you'd get something out of it, like money and a nice place to live, people to like you even if they don't like you. So then I look around my trailer and think that if the devil were in me, I'd be better off than I was.

Then I think that maybe there's a little devil in all of us. I think that sometimes, when someone's mean to me for no reason, just because they can be, that they're just doing it to get away with it, because they want to and because they can. Because that's what they want when no one's looking, is to be mean to me and get away with it. You don't want to be one of those people they can get away with it on, but I see it.

Just for example.

Like back when I was working with my Mom, landscaping, and she brought us to this big house outside Toronto, and she told me the guy wanted a line of trees along the side of his front yard, so the neighbours couldn't see him from their driveway. Well, the trees were going right along the edge of that driveway, just as far as he was legally allowed to put them at their current size, but you know they were going to get bigger. Mom said, when I said something about it, that the guy didn't even think about that. He just wanted some trees that were bushy and affordable, and he wanted us to put them in the ground. Rich people always tell you they can't afford something when they can, they just don't want to. He wanted to pay enough to have his front yard out of sight of the neighbour's driveway, but he didn't want to pay enough for big enough trees for it to happen right now, so he got these smaller trees that in a couple of years would do the trick. I pictured him inside the house, looking out the front window, thinking about how he'd got a good deal and how in a couple of years the investment would pay off. I thought about how he didn't account for how some of those trees would just die, because that's what trees do sometimes when you put them in city ground too close to the asphalt, just like people just like anything alive.

I thought about how he probably wasn't one of the ones who would let us come in and use the bathroom and drink his tap water, even though we'd be there all day.

I was going to dig the holes and put those trees in, while Mom was doing something else. Well, it took all day, and thank goodness I didn't have to pee from all the sweating, but I dug the holes, and I put them in, and I piled up the dirt a bit around the trunk just like she taught me, and I got the hose out and started watering, because when you plant trees, they always need a lot of water to get started, a little encouragement growing their roots out from where they were stuck in the pot for so long—rootbound.

I still maintain that when you're planting trees along someone's driveway, there's no way you're not going to get some dirt on that driveway, no matter how careful you are. So while I was thinking about this guy and how he didn't want to pay for trees as tall as he really wanted, I wasn't thinking about the guy he was trying to use them to get away from, but there I'd got dirt all over his driveway, little as there was. (Because I was careful digging, and the rule is you dig the dirt on the property you're working on, so that's where I put the piles of dirt I dug out, on that guy's side, but even so, there was a little on the other). Judging from what I thought about the guy who'd bought the trees, I just assumed the guy next door couldn't be as bad, but I was wrong. I stepped on his driveway for maybe five minutes so that I could aim the hose at the dirt on the edge of his drive, put my finger over the end of it to get some pressure going, aim it down so I could drive that dirt back where it came from.

Standing on his driveway, aiming back at the trees where I was working, I even thought that he'd appreciate how careful I'd been and how I cleaned up after. But then

I saw his car backing in from the road. I hadn't finished what I'd been doing, so I thought maybe he'd just stop and let me clean up; after all, it was a long enough driveway for him to stop and let me finish cleaning up, but then I saw him look at me in the rearview mirror, and I swear to fucking god he sped the fuck up. It just didn't make sense with the lay of the land, because at the back of the driveway, there were big giant cement pots where he kept his own trees, his own plants, his own work for someone else like me to do. Surely, he wouldn't want to back into them and after all, people just in general *slow down* before they come to a stop, so it would only make sense that coming in the driveway, he would slow down and come to a stop, first because that's what people do, and second because accelerating might well land his car crumpled by his own big cement pots when he couldn't stop in time.

But thank goodness for those big cement pots, because the space in between them was where I jumped before he got to me. In between them, with my hose, I watched him get out of the car and look at me, cursing me with his eyebrows for being a little too quick, when he thought he could have killed me and probably got away with it. After all, people don't care about people like me, and he was in his own driveway, and if you can't kill someone in your own driveway, where can you kill them? Only after he disappeared inside did I come out and wonder why he wouldn't let me finish the job. How there'd still be dirt under his car now for a long time, because I couldn't get to it anymore with how he parked. How now even if it rained, it wouldn't wash that dirt out from where it was.

So you see why I might think that the devil's more in that guy than in me, but I'd be wrong about that too.

Maybe the devil doesn't want me to have the things that that guy has, because he doesn't want me to think that I should get to run down people like me doing their jobs.

Maybe the devil wants me to be a good person.

If so, he has a funny way of showing it.

Mom didn't tell me where we were when we went to a property, just what to do when we got out of the van. But I could see the street signs on the corner, and I knew about how far we'd come and in what area we were, so when I got home, I wrote down in my journal:

There's a bad man at the corner of Forrester and Caldwell, near outside Toronto.

I thought it'd be enough to find him again, if I wanted.

I'd recognize him by how much he hated me.

2

Mom quit landscaping because she died, and so did I. I got a job at a restaurant. I met Brian. I liked working somewhere with a roof. Shade from the sun. I liked standing up for most of the job. I used to bend over a lot, and now I don't. I notice in my hips and in my ankles. My hips are better off even though my ankles swell now more. There's always got to be something wrong with what you're doing.

I'm happy not to landscape anymore. There was too much sunscreen. There was always a spot missed that would turn into a burn and then a tan, or it would just come off at some point during the day or if you touched some part too closely. Then people would look at you for the rest of the summer and know you work outside. They make their assumptions. But now it's one less that I'm inside. I work at the restaurant in the trailer park. It's hot in the summer without air conditioning, and people can still tell you work there, because they see you working there, but once you're gone, they can't tell you were there.

There are customers, and they speak to me. They never did that landscaping. No one sees or talks to the landscapers.

Even so, you could tell by the smell if I came off shift and went straight anywhere. It's the grease from the fryers that'll sink into your clothes and give you away. *French fries...* someone will say, and then they know you work a fryer. The only way to get rid of it is dish soap, which makes sense. It takes the grease from the dishes and the grease from my restaurant clothes just as well. I don't think I need to use it on my skin and my hair. I don't think. I'm always finding out new ways someone will find something out to hold against you. It seems like they just know.

Cheryl hired me when I was 14, because I walked in and asked for a job. But she didn't always have work for me at first, because of Vicky. Vicky had the job before I did, but Cheryl used to complain that Vicky would just stick around as long as it took to make enough money to drink as much as she wanted for a while, and then she wouldn't show up one day and then not for the rest of the week either. So I'd come in when Vicky was drinking, but Cheryl couldn't fire her, because Vicky had dated her grandson once for a while, and Cheryl had always felt poorly about that. Eventually, Vicky got a better job and quit coming in all together, but she still thought I somehow stole the job from her.

Stole the job and the grandson. I didn't want either of them, actually, but Jordie showed up just when Mom moved us into the trailer park, and I thought hey, I'm a trailer park person now, might as well become one. So when he asked if I wanted to take a walk down by the lake, I thought I'd better pretend to know where that was and what it meant. Apparently, it meant making out with Jordie down by the lake on the single bench the park could afford to put there, trying to make it seem more like the cottages a little farther down the shore. Like we were all just enjoying the lake and not withering in our souls. I guess a lot of people walk down by the lake to pretend that's not the case, because Vicky showed up and yelled at us. I didn't know they were together then. I don't know if Jordie knew either. I knew for sure I didn't want to date him, so I told him because of Vicky it couldn't happen again.

But I was a trailer park person after that.

For a while, I was a waitress, with Cheryl's daughter—Jordie's mom. It was the two of us out front and Cheryl in the kitchen, with Jackson if he was there that weekend doing the dishes. I was really good at remembering the orders, but I wasn't as good at the people. Sometimes they would try to tell me I messed up their order when I knew I didn't, and I'd tell them so. So one day I started drifting into the kitchen to help Cheryl out with the cooking. First it was a breakfast shift, and while she worked the grill and the fryers, I started making toast. I'd wait my tables too, but when I had a second, I'd come back in the kitchen and make the toast. I'd look over her head at the orders and figure out which toast went with which breakfast and just make it. Then when that went well, I got my own little grill. Toast and French toast. Toast and French toast and pancakes. Omelettes. Then garlic bread and grilled cheese at lunch hour. Grilled sandwiches. Reubens and patty melts. Then salads. When the right order came in, Cheryl could go on break, and she discovered she liked that.

Then it was my kitchen.

It was good for Cheryl. She'd been working this restaurant since before her husband died. He was here too, when she hired me. What an asshole. They both had to run the restaurant, because he did something with their retirement money I'll never know. But in the aftermath, they took on the restaurant. The restaurant was always a burden to someone, someone who didn't want to work after their retirement but had to anyway for the money. Manual labour into their seventies and eighties. The restaurant was owned by the trailer park, and every year at a board meeting they'd decide who was going to run it, keep the snowbirds fed over the summer months. They'd have to keep the prices low, but they wouldn't pay any rent, and they'd get to keep the profits, as long as they made sure that there were amenities here for everyone who lived in the park or came here in the summer. I say it's a restaurant, but actually there's an arcade in the back, a general store for the things people forgot when they drove to their weekend trailers, a craft area for the old ladies to sell knitted dish cloths and hand-made wreaths. The craft shop doesn't do much business, because all the old ladies make the same things; they don't need to buy them from someone else. But when one of the weekenders forgets a dish cloth, I get to write a note to keep under the counter, tell them about their profits the next time they come in for breakfast. *Frieda, blue scrubby, $2.*

The old ladies were better than the weekenders. They would have two trailers, one up here and one down in Florida, and they'd go back and forth every year. The weekenders were real people. They lived out of town in houses, but they bought a trailer because they thought it would be nice to have for the long weekends. The kind of people who, when something at their real house wore out or went out of fashion, would take it to the cottage, as they called it. The cottage was a trailer too, just owned by better people than the rest of us. Better people than the snowbirds. They and I both lived in trailers year-round, even if they had two and I only had the one. We had a lot more in common than I had with the weekenders.

They kept my secrets.

Mom bought the trailer when she last got divorced on the logic that she was going to get half a house's worth of money in the division of assets, so she'd buy half a house back. There was still a mortgage on it when she died. But so long as the payments kept coming in, there was no reason for the bank or anyone else to question whether anyone had the right to live there. So long as the bills kept getting paid, there was no reason to cut off the utilities. So long as I kept making it to school enough of the time, there was no reason to check in and make sure that everyone's parents were still alive.

The assumption wasn't right—that I needed someone to take care of me, and that without my mother, I wouldn't be fine. I was fine. I was more than fine. I didn't have anyone to take care of anymore. Actually, I found myself with a little less work to do. The water bill went down.

The old ladies knew, because they heard about it and talked about it, just like we always do when someone dies here. We talk about what happened, whether it was an accident, how they did it, and why. I think they felt the same way I did when it happened.

A little relieved.

A little concerned too, but just because of the change that was involved. But you know we always have ways of not being concerned for others, especially if being concerned would put us out any. So when after a while it was clear that I was still showing up for work, showing up for school, paying the bills, brushing my hair and putting on my eyeliner, the concern dissipated. And I felt free to live my life. Not that I wanted to live this way forever. Just until I graduated high school, and then I'd get student loans and live near a school, and no one would know where I'd come from, because by then I'd be able to scrub the smell off.

If I had to, I'd use the dish soap and buy a $2 scrubby from Frieda. If it would help slough off the skin the grease had gotten into.

When they show people working with meat, it's always the blood they try to emphasize, like it's the blood that's going to bother you, get into your skin and stain your clothes. It's not the blood. It's the fat. The fat from ground meat's what I wear home at the end of the night.

The old people might have actually preferred frozen food; some of them were weird like that, but the fact of the matter was that we couldn't afford the markup on it, so we made everything from scratch. It was Friday, and Friday means special. Special means we put something new up on the whiteboard and sell it until it runs out. Cheryl's daughter Molly went to an Italian restaurant in town and said we should make Italian wedding soup, that they give it out there, that it can't be that much to make. Just some chicken broth and a frozen block of spinach, little bits of pasta. Tiny little meatballs.

I'd been rolling tiny meatballs for about an hour now, and it wasn't about to end. There's no blood to notice in ground meat, but the fat starts to melt on your hands and forms a coating, like you're rubbing your hands in oil after a while, but an oil that smells like death. I was concerned it would make my living flesh smell like dead flesh, but that's no reason to stop. Molly said that the meatballs were *tiny*, and Cheryl agreed that if they were, they'd go further, so they'd be tiny. The volume of meat you need for a tiny meatball goes down by a factor of 3.14159 with the decrease in radius, so a tiny meatball doesn't use much meat at all, actually, which means the meat I've got left to get through doesn't seem to be getting any less. I thought about how much they'd have to pay me to roll the meatballs versus how much they might have had to pay for canned or frozen soup, and it worked out.

I'm still a deal.

What I know for sure is that I can't tell Molly the soup was a bad idea, because sometimes she talks to spirits out loud as she works, and sometimes she talks to the devil, and I don't want her to know that I'm the one that brought him around.

3

Brian is picking me up after work, but thank fuck I didn't meet him there. I met him at school. He wouldn't fit anywhere into the categories of people I'd made up to sort out the restaurant and trailer park people. I hope never to find out. If he were any of them, he'd probably be a weekender, but I couldn't see that happening either. If Brian were going to go somewhere for a weekend, he wouldn't go to a trailer and call it a cottage. Brian knows where I live and where I work, and that's enough.

And he knows he's not allowed to show up earlier than half an hour after the end of my shift, so I have time to walk home and shower.

That's the other thing about the restaurant; it's so close to home. I'm not driving around for hours not getting paid for travel time like when we were landscaping. It's only a few minutes down the block.

The first thing I thought when I saw Brian at school was *housecat*. Because I'm a feral cat without the resources to really clean myself up like him. Nice clothes. Money for hair products. He didn't earn any of it. His parents paid.

They asked him, when he was going out, if he needed any money, and he'd say yes, and they'd give it to him. Can you imagine? I couldn't. Not even when my mom was alive would that ever happen. I've always found my own money. Or else not eat or not wear clothes, and neither of those are good options. You learn to be cheap in ways Brian would never have to figure out. *Housecat.*

If I could be like him, though, I would. Hang around him long enough, learn something about how it's done, and be like him. I don't know if he noticed the vast difference it made, where our money came from and what we had to do for it.

I know that he didn't comment on where I lived and that if it ever seemed I felt off about it, he'd make sure I knew he didn't care. He *really didn't care*, and that means something, because one of the things you start to notice when you live where I live is how often people say things like "Oh yeah, his cousin lives in a trailer," as if it's a character deficiency and not just by happenstance the dwelling that they're paying off after their mother offed themselves, hoping to make it through long enough to get a high school diploma before abandoning it and their whole life besides. Like there's something you could assume about people who lived in them.

It just didn't occur to Brian to think that way. And he'd already made plans to come with me when I left. We made plans.

On my way out the door, I passed the box that my mother always called my hope chest. She said it was a thing people did for girls when they were young, make a chest full of household items they would need when they were married, give it to them after the wedding. She talked in the abstract about making one for me and got a pretty big cardboard box and said that that was it. We drove to the Walmart, and I bought two cast-iron pans in different sizes with the money I'd made that day at the restaurant, and we put them in the box. There they still were.

I made Brian meet me in the driveway. He didn't need to see that.

He's too good for it.

I like his hair and how deep his voice is. I like how while I was working, he'll have been looking up new bands, saving songs to show me when I get in the car and as we drive around. Brian really likes this place in town where they've got a restaurant, a café, a movie theatre and a bookshop all in the same building, and we'll go to all of them. Split a pizza at the restaurant, baked in a wood oven, the thin crust that gets those huge air pockets. He'd insist that he didn't watch movies, only films. I liked looking through the books with him, but mostly the classics and film sections, talking about which ones we already had and which ones we could loan each other. Neither of us liked to loan them, so if you loaned them, that was a bad sign already. It meant the book had to be read, but it wasn't actually all that good. It wasn't worth protecting. When Brian loaned me albums, he'd take the liner notes out of them, to make sure he got them back. You can't do that to Nabokov, which is why we had our own of each of them. He bought me *The Marilyn Encyclopedia* for my birthday because, "You remind me of her," and I took that to mean that it was a good reason to love me that I should embody.

I liked going home at the end of the night and putting a new book on my dresser, reading it in bed, putting it away after on a shelf that I had learned to put up on the wall above my bed for just that purpose. One nice thing in here to remind me of who I could be out there.

Tonight, we decided to linger at the café, get dessert after our pizza. I knew that it would double how much the check would be and that I'd have to pay for it, but I also knew that thinking about things like that was something only people worse than Brian would think about, so I couldn't say anything or even let on. I had two days' cash wages from the restaurant in my wallet, and that was enough to cover it and probably a book, but I couldn't put away anything for the end of the month. At this point, though, there were a lot more days of the month, so I could make it up at some point.

I came out of the bookshop with a hardback copy of *The Brothers Karamazov* and when I showed him, Brian said to me, "That is a precious object. Don't loan it out."

I felt good about that.

We drove around a little, listening to Brian's music, not talking. It was comfortable. We'd usually drive out to this little spot on the edge of town, a parking lot in a plaza with not much else in it but us, and then Brian would turn off the car, and we would talk about important things. I think that's where he was taking me.

The devil made me think that one of these days, out there, I'd kill him. That while we both had pocketknives, he wouldn't think to use his like I would, wouldn't see it coming, so that I'd pull mine out first and cut him before he knew what was happening. But not today.

Brian said he had something important to talk about, and I knew he wasn't breaking up with me, so there wasn't much left it could be. So when he came out with it, I wasn't at all surprised, and I always knew what was going to happen there, but I didn't say anything out loud, because I knew that Brian worked on a different set of concepts than I did about the matter, that he thought these things were important when they weren't, that the way he thought about these things was influenced by how he'd been raised differently than I had, with the idea that people loved you and that you could love them back. I expected him to phrase it like a question, like he had on our first date, when he pulled me into the alleyway and asked politely, "Can I kiss you?" And I told him that he didn't need to do that. Maybe that's what he was thinking when he came out with a statement instead, not a question, but a statement. A proposition under the guise of an opinion. Brian parked the car and after a long enough time to make it clear that what he was saying was significant, Brian finally came out with it:

"I think we should have sex."

It was a proposal, not a statement or an expectation or any of the things that were about to happen being said out loud, like it had always been. And I knew that he was different because, unlike those boys before him, Brian was asking.

I thought about my role and how best to play it plausibly, what Brian might expect, but the situation had played out so many times before in my imagination that I knew, I already knew how I had to behave from here on, and I told him I'd have to think about it.

He nodded to say of course and told me how excited Nick Cave was to get an email from Leonard Cohen.

4

I knew I'd have to *think about it* for a few days, for the sake of appearances. But I always knew this question would happen and what to do about it. I knew that once I declared my decision aloud, things were going to change. We'd have to start making plans. I'd tell Brian that I'd started taking birth control (which I'd been on all along), and worst of all I knew that I'd have to let him in my home. I knew I'd have to get rid of some more of Mom's things, clear the space around the path she made so I could get to my bed from the door, rest up, get back out—another day.

When Brian dropped me off, I went inside and instead of feeling the sudden loss of humanity that I usually felt when I was alone after a period when I wasn't, I filled the void with imagined futures of Brian coming in and being welcome. I looked around and catalogued the changes I'd have to make. I started a fire in the woodstove to save a bit on heating costs. The propane only kicked in when it got below a certain temperature, so I could save money on it by not letting that temperature happen. Otherwise, if I didn't burn wood in addition to the propane, and it was cold, the heat would cost about $7 a day.

And then there was the money I'd spent earlier. I'd have to run the woodstove for a *while* to make that up. I couldn't afford $210 for heat along with $300 for maintenance fees for the park, a telephone bill and internet, water and electricity. The maintenance fees had doubled since the new manager had come in. She was one of them and didn't understand that the people who were here were here because they didn't have that kind of money. She'd say things like, *Don't you want it to be nice?* Like she thought that everyone had the option of nice things and some of us just didn't choose them for no good reason except no one had thought to suggest it.

You're killing me, Christie, I thought as I packed the woodstove with kindling, soft and hardwood. Eventually, the wood pile out back would diminish, and I'd have to either replace it or use the propane all the time. It was one of the nice things my mother had left behind for me, something to burn, some warmth. She'd collect wood from people who were cutting down trees from their properties, offer to take it away for free, cut it into small enough pieces at their houses to drag away, and then cut it into smaller pieces again outside here in the yard, just small enough for the stove. The wood had to dry out; you couldn't burn it green, or there'd be smoke, and it wouldn't burn well. Once it's dry, it's dry, and doesn't really wet again, even in the rain. You can burn wet wood if it's wet from rain but not if it's wet from being green. You can learn a lot of things by burning things.

Brian hadn't fucked anyone before, but I had, and he knew it. That's why I was waiting for this question to come around. He tried to play it up like he'd had so many chances but always turned them down, waiting for the right person, he said, but I could tell that's what he was doing, playing it up. Someone who looked like him and who was raised that way didn't have that many opportunities and if they did, they took them. I knew that about males. It's the female who decides when mating will occur, they told us in biology.

I could have brought it up myself, but there's also a judgement a male makes when you do that and besides, I didn't want to.

I wanted him to be a good person.

Whatever I meant by that.

Me, I lost my virginity to some boy in the woods the weekend after my best friend when I was 13 told me she had. I thought to myself, huh, might as well, and then I found someone to do it with. We hung out a lot in the woods back then, drinking forties and smoking other people's weed. Sometimes we'd buy ecstasy or acid or mushrooms and make a night of it, but usually we'd just show up and see who was there worth talking to. Sometimes if there was a boy there we liked, she'd make out with him or I would, or we both would. I miss Alison. So when she said she fucked some guy one night when I wasn't around, I went out and found one of those boys and took his hand from where we were, sitting on the tree stumps, pulled him farther into the forest and put a condom in his hand. After that, I didn't have to do much except tell him I didn't want to be his girlfriend. That's what they always try to do, when you let them fuck you, get some kind of promise from you that it might happen again, and maybe again after that. But that wasn't what it was about.

After that there were a few more boys, most of them around my age, some of them a little older, never older than 25. I had fun with them, until one of them did it in a way that wasn't fun, and then I stopped that, stopped going to the woods, stopped seeing Alison, started staying home a lot, reading books by the fire. When I met Brian at school, I thought it could be different, because I'd never met a boy at school, let alone one I knew would graduate, who had a life plan and a college fund. Brian said there was enough there that we both could go to university, live together, save money that way, make it work, even if I had nothing to offer.

He said he didn't care about money, but I still wondered how much he'd care when one night it was my turn to pay the bill and I couldn't.

So far it hadn't happened, but it might.

The devil in me said that going to university with Brian was a kind of death, that I'd have to give up too much of myself to make space for him in some tiny apartment on a college campus where I'd have to pretend that my mom had our dinners catered when she was too tired to cook, like his did.

I would make this trailer nice to take Brian's virginity.

5

When I was younger, my music teacher always wanted me to join the band, because I was the only one who played the trombone and not only could I do the bass for the regular band, she had a jazz band going that needed me too. She thought, like they always do, that I didn't sign up because I didn't want to. But then one day she asked me please to join the band, and I told her why I couldn't. Why I had to go home on the bus each day, not stay behind, because if I stayed behind, then I couldn't get home at all. Then that music teacher called my mom and said something and from then on, after class, I stayed behind and played in the band, and when I got done adding the bass notes to her songs, I'd stay behind at the front of the room, standing near her desk while everyone else left and she packed up, and then she'd drive me home in a minivan, and she'd let me sit in the front seat. Every time I was ashamed to be there, and every time when I got home, my Mom would explain that if that woman wanted me in her school band, she'd have to do something for it, make the drive, when by then I knew it was a cover story.

All that time I wouldn't talk, because I didn't know what was going on, until one day Mrs. Nemeth turned to me in the right seat of her van and said, "Just say something! Say the first word that comes to mind!" And I said, finally, "trimester", and she asked, "Why did you say that?" and I told her, "Because I heard it on the radio, and I don't know what it means." At which point she explained to me that when a woman is pregnant, they divide the pregnancy into three temporal periods, and I resolved never to speak again, now ashamed for one that I hadn't known, and ashamed for another for having been born. The next week, when she told me to speak, I said, "No," which I think should have counted, but it didn't.

6

When I got to work the following morning, Cheryl had already let some people inside. They knew we didn't open until 8, but the seniors liked to have their breakfast earlier, closer to when they'd gotten up. They didn't think about the person who would have to be there an hour earlier than whenever they felt like eating, to clean the floors and set the ashtrays out on the tables, get the ketchup bottles out of the fridge, precook the bacon by half so it wouldn't take as long when the orders came in. Pressure cook the hash browns so we could fry them to order without worrying if they were hard in the middle.

They thought they were making some kind of moral point by being here early, like if they did it often enough we'd realize that we should just be open, always be open, always be available and ready and have everything ready and on and good, in case one of them wanted a cup of coffee *fucking immeeeeediately* and without waiting the final 15 minutes it would take for us to actually be ready to open. I told Cheryl she should draw a hard line and if she weren't here, they would just wait on the deck until 8 until they figured out they shouldn't. But Cheryl was nice and always let them in, as long as she was there to do it, which put us behind on breakfast because instead of doing all the prep work, we had to set them up at a table, make the coffee, pour the cream into those little metal pourers. Guess how much each table would use because, once the cream was on the table, you couldn't take it back because of health regulations. It was still cheaper than those little individual creamers you could also get at the restaurant supply.

Fuck people who feel entitled to another person's time. Like they'd earned it somehow. Someone else's hours, and the argument was always the same and always the worst—that if you didn't want to be treated like that, you shouldn't be where you are in life, do what you do, be who you are, be born to whom you were born to.

I quick peeled some potatoes, cut them down to hash-brown size, put them in the pressure cooker. Laid the bacon out on the grill while Cheryl made small talk with the people who were making her suffer, poured their coffees and when they said, "just half," she poured two-thirds, pretend that it's an accident. Because if you don't do that, they always *always* look at a real half and say, "maybe a little more." It was always maybe a little more with those people.

Molly came in at 8 like she was supposed to. Cheryl would have picked her up the night before. She lived out of town with her kids and came in on the weekends, stayed with Cheryl, served tables, brought a paycheck home to town where her kids went to school. Jordie wasn't here, but Jackson was; he'd come in later, do some dishes. Molly would take some money out of our tip jar and give it to him before he ran off again. At the end of the day, she'd forget she'd done it and split up the money just as if it were all there, half for each of us. I wouldn't say anything about it.

On a busy morning, we'd get into a pattern, and we wouldn't have to talk at all, except to say "behind you" when we were. That's when the job was easiest. Molly brought the orders in and hung them on the line. I'd watch what Cheryl was cooking on the stove and the grill and make my parts of the order on the other side of the kitchen, ensuring that whatever I needed to make was ready when she needed it to be. Molly would pop back into the kitchen and pick up the plates, take them back out to the tables. There was no smoking in the kitchen, so she'd leave her burning cigarette on the front counter, the one that separated us from them, staff from customers, and kept them all on their proper side, except for the impertinent ones who thought that sometimes Molly was too slow with the coffee refills and decided to help themselves. I think they did it sometimes because they wanted to help her out a little. But also sometimes they did it because they resented the power we had over them, deciding when and how they'd have their hot drinks. Sometimes I think they got a kick out of coming behind the counter, like they were playing one of us, one of the special few behind the counter people. But it wasn't a life they wanted to live forever.

Some people might resent other people play acting their lives, but I'm trying to think of other things.

Brian and the future.

I told him I couldn't see him tonight, and I didn't say why. This was part of the experience I was making for him, the anticipation before I told him that I'd thought about it, and he could stick his dick in me if he wanted.

There are two shifts of breakfast, one where the old people eat as early as possible, and the second when the younger people get up, come down, and keep asking me if we still have breakfast, up until about 2pm. That's when everyone clears out, and I can peel and pressure cook more potatoes for mashed. It's only happened a couple of times that someone comes back and asks for breakfast at dinner, at which point Cheryl panics because we don't have any hash browns, and she wouldn't consider serving the special with some other form of potato instead or even charging more for it because of it was dinner.

The potatoes come once a week from a farm an hour out of town. Cheryl makes the trip with Jackson, and he pretends that carrying the bags in from the car is the worst thing that's happened to anyone, the hardest work anyone has ever done. Cheryl pays him from the cash register, and he leaves for an hour to buy weed. Then I carry the bags the rest of the way in from the entranceway where Jackson left them.

Molly was muttering to herself again, but the orders still kept coming in and going out, and that meant it wasn't important. I'm keeping up with the dishes until Jackson gets here, but we do them in a sink the old-fashioned way, and we're not allowed to use towels to dry them because of health regulations, so some of the plates are still wet when we put the food back on them and send them out again. Nobody seems to care.

Everything's going fine, and I'm looking forward to an evening of throwing things in the fire that don't need to be in my trailer anymore, when somewhere near the end of my shift, Molly looks past me and says, "Watch it!"

I ask her what's behind me, and she tells me not to worry.

"Your soul is old enough already," she says.

When everyone's cleared out for the night, I take some money out of my pay for the day and put it back in the till, take a pack of cigarettes from the shelf. Take them down to the bench by the lake and smoke them with vodka. The security guard stops by to make sure I haven't got a fire going. That's against park policy, but I haven't got a fire going, so they can't get me for it.

On the other side of the lake, I heard the devil scream.

7

Every stairway has a shadow.
There are no other ways through.
It's not a pebble in your pocket.
Its own weight wears it down.

I tell Brian at school. He sticks his tongue in my mouth and I like it, even with how wet it is. He should know better. He's been told before we're not supposed to go too hard in the hallways. The vice principal called him in and told him. She didn't say anything to me. Likely because I had a habit of arguing with them. The office people.

It's hard to believe in authorities that are usually either wrong or dead.

Brian seemed so happy, and the devil told me it was because he'd heard that I was this kind of girl and that he'd just found out that all the time he'd put in so far was worth it. I laughed back at him, because I knew I wasn't worth all that much to anyone who wasn't, for some fucking reason, already in love with me.

I knew Brian loved me, and he knew I loved him too, and the devil knew I'd hurt him anyway.

8

People assume that when someone dies, you're going to stop what you're doing, tell everyone, make a big deal out of it. The police assumed that's what I would do, too. But you don't have to do that. You don't have to make it so everyone you talk to is sad, full of pity, concerned for your welfare, meddling. You can carry on like nothing happened.

Maybe nothing did happen.

She always said she would use a gun if she did it, but she lied.

She was too concerned about staying pretty. What men thought.

If I told her what she looked like dead, she would have been so embarrassed.

It's fine to put natural materials in the woodstove; that's just fuel. Artificial materials will add too much to the creosote, she said, and then when the creosote gets too hot, the chimney sets on fire. That can damage the metal, as the thin sheets disintegrate, letting the flames into the house through barely perceptible cracks that, at some point, fall apart.

So I burned some artificial materials in the firepit in the backyard. Acrylic clothes and home décor. Mom thought when she built it that we might spend evenings out back, watching the fire, I don't know what else. It was made of bricks that she salvaged from someone's property, stacked up in an interlocking pattern that would let the fire breathe a little while keeping it contained. We never used it, then I did.

Some other things, it was worth walking them down to the dumpsters. About three-quarters of a kilometre from the trailer were the park's dumpsters. You weren't supposed to use more of them than your fair share. If you wanted to dispose of large items, you were on your own. Or you could burn them out back while the neighbours pretended you didn't, assumed you don't know what you're doing, you're too young, they're not all that attached to the air anyway. It's not any worse than anything else that's always happening.

I burned newspapers and magazines in the woodstove, despite the thick and coloured inks. They burned quickly and produced a lot of ashes, but they weren't worth carrying to the dumpsters or burning out back. I burned the old couch in pieces I hacked apart with the wood axe we used to use to make the firewood small enough for the stove. I brought some clothes to the dumpster, but I didn't want to throw them quite in. Someone might make use of them yet. I tucked parts of them in with the trash and let the rest hang over the sides, on display like a shop window. Her date night dresses; her wedding dresses; a few good work shirts that were actually men's. Something for everyone.

I got the work done over the course of a few nights, separating my burn piles into indoor and outdoor, carrying what I could on foot to the dumpsters after dark. You'd think that it would be suspicious, walking to the dumpsters after dark three nights in a row, but actually people do things in the dark because no one is up and the people who are up aren't looking. There's a reason for it. I reasoned that if I saw anyone, it would likely be one of my co-conspirators, and that they'd be just as motivated as I was not to ask what I was doing.

After three nights of this, by the time Brian appeared at the door, I'd forgotten that the purpose of all this wasn't just to clean the trailer, and I remembered the indelible mark that I'd leave on this boy's psyche was, at this point, pretty much inevitable, and I smiled thinking of how in some small way I'd figured out how to have an effect on the world that otherwise wouldn't have me. He appeared at the door in a full suit—black pants, black blazer, white shirt, black tie (thin)—his back facing me as I opened it. But when he heard the door open, he spun around and revealed that he was holding a single flower, that he raised to his face, his eyebrows raising over it. He had an angular face that directed your eyes toward the bottom of it, where the carnation was currently raised to his lips. From the way he moved, I could tell he was imitating something he'd once seen in a film, even if I didn't get the reference. It was clear that he'd put a lot of thought into this look, that he'd imagined in advance what it would look like from my point of view, that he'd acquired the suit, the prop flower, did his hair. He was thinking about this experience and my perspective of it, anticipating what I'd see and what its effect would be. He was doing something for me. It was a far cry from the chivalry I'd encountered in the forest, when a boy would either take his t-shirt off and put it down on the ground for you to lay on as he fucked you, or he wouldn't.

"You came," I said.

"Of course?" he laughed.

We both laughed.

I'd forgotten at some point that this wasn't all about me and my home, that actually, he'd be here too, and whenever he was here, everything was better. It was something I'd have to learn to rely on, make a point of it. I could see how life might be better with that assumption. But I was also worried that having made that assumption, it would be worse when he discovered what I was and that he was better off without me.

I took Brian's pink carnation, snipped the end at an angle and filled a glass halfway with water. I set it down on the table that defined the kitchen area; without that table, it wasn't clear where the kitchen ended and the living room began. I didn't want Brian sitting at the kitchen table, though, so I blocked him. We can't end up sitting at opposite ends of the table.

Not on virginity day.

As he advanced farther and farther into my trailer, about 15 feet in all, I thought about all of the things he could notice, but I also saw that he didn't seem to be noticing them, like he actually didn't care. And I remembered he was Brian, and that's why I thought he loved me. Brian who engaged with me as a human would, who didn't seem to have an immediate sense of my inferiority, and who wouldn't hold whatever it was that I thought he might see against me, whether it was the calcium that I couldn't quite remove from the ends of the taps, the dinginess of the ceiling tiles because the man who had owned this place before my Mom did had chain-smoked cigars in it for 20 years, or the carpet that I'd just glued down into place after a corner had started lifting. If he didn't step in that exact spot (and who steps in corners), the only indicator was the faint scent of glue.

Brian stumbled past me, took his jacket off and sat cross-legged on the bed, like he would if we were at his own house. Like the fact that I had a bed and he had a bed meant we were just the same, and maybe that is what it meant. Just like we were at his house and not stuck in my head attempting to reconcile how far he'd been displaced from his natural environment.

What kind of a foreign experience he must be having now. How different he was.

Brian kissed me and asked if it was all right if he took my shirt off. He helped me loosen his tie and pull it over his head, then I undid each of his buttons as he sat there, shoulders up while his arms pressed against the mattress at each of his sides. I wondered at what he might be thinking, and I thought of my ex who had told me that after we fucked for the first time, he found me more attractive, and he phrased it like a general theory, where fucking someone makes them hotter. And I wondered if Brian's perception of my home was in that way coloured by the fact that I had already agreed to fuck him, and this is where it would happen. And if that was the case, he'd never know the cold and empty home that I had here, what it had been like first with a dead woman and a dead woman's things, and how hard I had to try to keep it if not bad, at least not any worse than it was.

But I wanted him not to know that. I wanted him to so desperately, because while Brian and I were getting toward a point where he'd be sticking his dick in me, I knew that it would be a significant event for him, that it hadn't been for me, and that there was no way it could have been, and I felt an acute sense of longing for what he was experiencing now, as a life that I never could have led. The same sort of acute sense of loss whenever it really becomes something to feel—that I could have been born better but just wasn't.

Brian took the crucifix from around my neck and hung it from the bedpost. He said something that I always remembered: "I do want to marry you someday." I think he had to say it because he was Catholic, and Catholics aren't allowed to fuck. That little bit of insight into him, though, made all the difference, because I knew I wasn't all that had him (the church did too); nevertheless, here was a casual reference to an extreme sort of commitment that made me think that all of our plans might just happen. That everything that had happened before didn't matter, that now that I had him, and Brian had me, I could become him or at least something else than I was. I even thought, for a moment, *what if it all worked out, Brian's way?*

But the devil laughed.

We lay on the bed and without looking down, I signaled that it was time to remove pants by undoing the button on his, at which point he took over and removed the offending garment. I did mine as well and lay on the bed, naked, while Brian took a moment to glance over me in such a way that my discomfort was discordant with the loving manner he went about it.

Brian had read gynecology textbooks, he said, in preparation, and he attempted both manual and oral stimulation with some success. "You should masturbate," he told me, and I thought yeah, maybe. It didn't really seem an option when there were two of us living here in what was essentially one room, but now that I lived alone I guess it's once again an option. I told him I was on birth control, and he just believed me. And when he stuck it in, I felt all these things at once: a blooming, burning, sentimental love for the boy whom I was fucking; an anticipation for how our relationship would change, now that I had some concept of what this meant to him; an increasingly nuanced concept of my power, as I knew that he'd conceive of himself as losing something here that I had not, a non-reciprocal transaction where I'd *taken* his virginity, and where he'd perhaps even sacrificed himself for me. (I think the marriage proposal was meant to mitigate some concern of his breaking a covenant with the divine—for me. And that made me worry because whenever someone's done something for me, even if I didn't want them to, they seemed to think I still owed them, and the fact that there were so many of them that thought that way, I started to think maybe I did. How much for Brian's soul?)

As he thrust into me, I raised my hips back up to him as well as I could. I wanted him to grab my arms and hold them down by the wrists, like my ex had, like I was used to, but *no*, I told myself. We were kissing, and his sly tongue caught mine in a dance that made me think that this is what it's like to fuck someone you love, where things just kind of fit, and then he put his hand down on my clit and kept fucking, telling me that that's where all the nerve endings really were, but that women had been bred for chastity over generations resulting in a wider distance between the clit and the vagina that resulted in decreased sexual pleasure, unless, of course, someone used their hands. I felt a wave of warmth and an electric vibration moving through me and, as soon as I felt it, grabbed him and pulled him into me as far as I could, hitting cervix. I wrapped my legs around him and squeezed his cock with a kegel, and the sound he made could have been interpreted as either sexual pleasure or an outpouring of sorrow about the life he'd just conceived himself to have lost—the good life, the chaste life, where you don't fuck waitresses in their trailers. There was no way to determine which one it was, and by then I was distracted by a darkening spot on the back corner of the ceiling tile, where water was getting in and shifting the nicotine stains around, and that there was no way I could pay for that. I cried a little about how no matter how well I was doing here, there was always something to fall apart, and also about how sweet Brian had been and how I was now embedded in something I thought was doomed to fail but desperately hoped would not. Brian cried a little too, about how while he loved me, he'd still been told that good people don't fuck, and even though he'd wanted to, there were voices that told him he shouldn't have.

I felt the semen expand through my body, through my torso, knees and elbows and into my fingertips. I felt when it crossed the blood-brain barrier and made me worry even more I'd lose him, not only because of what I'd done and who I was, but also because of the devil in the water stain spreading across my ceiling tile.

Part Two

9

Something's living in the crawl space.
All signs point to animal.
The smell doesn't linger in winter.
No one smells it, not at all.

Brian and I started fucking all the time. We fucked at my trailer before going out for the evening and again when we'd come back. We fucked at his house when his parents weren't home in between him figuring out songs on his guitar. We fucked in his car when we were out, pulled over on a back highway dirt road; sometimes it was dark, and sometimes it wasn't. I blew him in the dark corner behind the vending machine area at school, and he fingered me on the bus we'd take to go to the record store in Toronto. We looked at knives, and I saw the look in his eye when I said I was going to use mine on him someday, not scared, never scared, just thrilled by the thought of doing something new, something literary, blood for aesthetic purposes.

I showered more often, after one day Molly leaned over at the counter to tell me that I smelled like I'd been ridden hard and put away wet. I thought it must be serious if she could smell it over the cigarettes we shared at the front counter, each one of us putting it down because we had to go back in the kitchen for something, and smoking wasn't allowed in the kitchen.

Health regulations.

The water bill went up a little bit.

Jackson didn't show up for work this weekend; when Cheryl went to pick him up with Molly, he said he had schoolwork to do and he'd stay behind on his own, and after a brief discussion about whether he could handle it on his own I guess she decided, fuck it. That move put me on dishes.

The dishes were a completely different job depending on what time of day it was. During the breakfast rush and the lunch rush and the dinner rush, when people keep coming and coming and coming, the dishes were an infinite stream of used food, half dry egg yolk and balled up napkins hiding between plates that someone had decided to helpfully stack themselves at the table. So when Molly picked them up, she wouldn't know that in between those plates there were scrambled eggs, a sausage, the tomato picked off a sandwich, napkins, bits of bread and congealed gravy, and anything else the customers were trying to hide from us. A part of the meal they didn't like or the receipts they finally cleaned out of their purse while at the table.

I differentiated between the surprises according to whether or not they'd dissolve in the dish water. There weren't any garbage disposals here; Christie had installed a new water waste system for the park that couldn't take that kind of water. She said the lagoon would be good for the whole park, and she charged us $1500 each to have it installed, decided on by vote at a meeting that nobody who lived here full-time could attend, because we didn't have the free time or the foresight to think that if we didn't go, we'd get so fucked over. So the bill came, and I paid it from Mom's death benefit, what was leftover after the cremation, but it meant I couldn't afford an urn, and there she was in the cardboard box she came in from Canada Post, tracked parcel. Christie took bids on contractors and went with the lowest one, which ultimately meant that the thing never worked right and after a little while, they shut it down, let it reek. They couldn't afford to get someone better to do the job right, and no one was going to put in another $1500, so instead, they paid someone who usually did septic tanks to come and empty it once in a while. At least that's what they charged us for in the maintenance fee increase.

Usually, I'd check between the dishes before I put them in the sink, but when the counter space was full, Molly'd come in and drop the stack directly in the sink. The breads might dissolve if the pieces were small enough. Pancakes disappeared. Pools of maple syrup made the water thicker and made my hands smell sweet, tempering the more disgusting bits of food that I'd have to pull out of the water by the handful. The garbage bin was a bag inside a box from which we'd pulled the most recent jug of fryer oil, and that way we could throw them out as necessary and not worry about cleaning them. The trash was full of wet napkins, handfuls of chopped vegetables soaked in dish water, meats that held together even if they'd once been ground.

All these textures in my hands meant trouble for the lagoon and that meant heavy wet trash sacks I'd drive down to the dumpsters at the end of the night in Cheryl's golf cart.

I thought about asking her to lend it to me back when I was cleaning Mom's stuff from the trailer, but I didn't want her asking if she could help.

The dishes at the end of the night were better. Those were the ones we'd made, cooking and serving and swiping mayo across the tops of buns, using the same knife all day and washing it once after breakfast, once after lunch, and now once when we were done. Those dishes were predictable, finite, ours because we'd used them, and didn't have any extras. Even the grease trap from the flat top where Cheryl scraped the oil after cooking something fatty was fine, because that's where the grease was supposed to go. I was expecting that, and I knew how to handle it.

In the middle of the afternoon, though, this woman Lorraine came in, excited because she'd won thousands on a scratch ticket. She said she wanted to celebrate with friends and asked if we'd stay open late. Cheryl normally didn't consider requests, but she thought maybe if we set a menu and did it like a caterer, it wouldn't be too much hassle to keep me and Molly behind, just a couple hours. She was sure that it'd be worth our while, because Lorraine wouldn't make a special request and at the same time announce that she'd got $50K on a BINGO scratcher if she didn't plan on making it worth all our whiles.

Right?

I told Brian that I couldn't come out that night and as I did, I worried what he'd do when I wasn't around, but I didn't really have a choice.

Come closing time, Lorraine came in with six of her old friends and told them all about how she'd got the whole place to themselves, that she'd made it so for them, that this was a private party. We wrote a simple menu on the whiteboard with the options that we knew they'd pick because they'd all been here so many times before. We kept out everything that we knew we'd need to make it, and Molly set them up at the table farthest from the counter with our cigarettes. She served one side of the table while I refilled drinks at the other, to show them how special an occasion it was, two servers and all, and then I'd run back to the kitchen to help Cheryl with the food. My feet hurt, but I thought of how much money I'd already spent that month and the look on Christie's face if I didn't come through with the maintenance fees, what it would mean if Lorraine would tip like she'd just won money. If there were $20 or $30 in it even, I could catch up on where I should be at for the month and not have to think about it anymore. But since Lorraine had asked us to stay open, I thought maybe more than the usual percent, because of all the trouble I thought maybe she'd take it upon herself to make it up to us, which in my case meant just something to catch up and maybe something else to get ahead, a couple of days not worrying about a couple of fucking dollars sounded awfully good to me, and I wanted it. I thought Lorraine must know how it feels to be on your feet for ten hours and then another few hours long after. I think she used to be a nurse and I heard once what happens to their ankles, and I wonder if that didn't happen to Lorraine and that's why she looked a little younger than most but still old enough to retire.

The order was full of "If I could just..."s, which is what I called the unreasonable requests that people would make under the guise that it was reasonable. "If I could just get coleslaw as a side instead of fries..." they'd say, not knowing that to do so I'd have to pull out the food processors and grind three heads of cabbage after we ran out of coleslaw at the end of the night like we always do. But we did it, because that was a lot of money and Lorraine would see everything and know what kind of effort we'd put in and how to compensate for it and, after all, she could afford it now.

And once the food was served, I could start on the back dishes, the ones we wouldn't need until tomorrow. I got through those and then the ones Molly brought back from the table as they finished. Dinner plates and cold drink cups, then coffee cups and small plates from apple pie with cheddar cheese, melted in the microwave, and a whole pot of decaf for Dave, who couldn't drink caffeine that late at night and didn't like tea.

By the time I turned around from the sink for more than just a second to grab something else to clean, Lorraine and her friends had gone, and Molly and Cheryl were sat down at a table, drinking what was left of the decaf, so it wouldn't go to waste. I went and sat down with them, and I asked straight out.

"How much did they tip?"

Cheryl shook her head, and I should see that Molly was tearing up a little, and I thought that maybe I'd sat down at the wrong time, they were talking about something serious, something familial. But they weren't.

Cheryl breathed in and out and in again before she said, "Nothing,"

"Fucking nothing," Molly said.

It was something about the hope Lorraine embodied and the novelty of it all that had made us all think that there was a chance we'd end up even slightly better instead of worse, have an extra $20 to go toward the propane instead of three extra hours of swollen ankles and three less hours to rest them before we all came back tomorrow, something about getting caught up in the excitement that made us think that when something good happened, it'd happen to all of us, something about the realization that if someone ever did make it in a big way, they'd forget ever having met us, deny they ever knew us, and just leave, take off and leave the rest of us to clean up after them, which we had to do because we were the ones still here and because we'd still be here the next day and the next. Because we knew it was better to clean up other people's dirt than it was to still have it around.

10

I woke up and smelled my hair. Fryer grease. I'd gotten into bed without showering, knowing that in the morning I'd have to wash the sheets, get up earlier. Reasoned that I'd have to clean them anyway, because of the semen stains, and that it was better to do it in the morning, so that I could hang them to dry and maybe put them back on the bed by evening, or else just use the sleeping bag bare I was using as a blanket, like people did when they used them to camp. I pulled the sheets off the bed and threw them in the tub, added water and some body wash, since I was out of detergent and I figured body wash would be just as good for getting out body stains (honestly I did it that way a lot and always thought the same way about it), let that soak while I made coffee. When I showered, I'd stamp the sheets around like I was trying to get the juice out of grapes for wine, then I'd sit on the side of the tub and pick out one end of the sheet, find the white spots, rub one part of the sheet against the other until they weren't visible anymore, keep going until I got to the other end of the sheet, like what would happen inside a washing machine I reasoned, if I had one, all those fabrics rubbing together, making the other ones cleaner instead of what the devil said happens when people rub together—those people get condemned to hell.

I drained the water after I shampooed my hair but before I conditioned it, so that the conditioner doesn't get on the sheets and recreate the stains. The devil watches the water disappearing from the bathtub and tells me quick to drink it before it's gone, but I won't do it. Another chance as I pick up the fabric and twist it in parts as best I can to get the water out, so that it'll dry quickly enough before being wet for so long makes it sour, makes it worse than when I started. Hang it on the line and hope it doesn't rain or get so cold it freezes.

I look forward to seeing Brian at school so I can be somebody else for a while.

Brian's voice is deep enough when he talks but when he sings, it's like he's pulling something up from underground, like the wavelength is a string that can't possibly begin anywhere but far under the earth, concentrating in him and then unleashed on the rest of us only in a dissipated form human ears could handle, but always with a sense of what it had been—echoes of the underworld. A lot of the time he wore white shirts with buttons, and he'd even put a jacket on top but you could tell by the shapes his body made underneath, he wasn't doing it as a capitalist. He looked like an artist someone put a suit on just to bring him out in public for a while, but also like he agreed to do it if only it was his own suit, this thing we'd picked up on consignment downtown, jeans instead of trousers. I could always tell where his dick was by his stance or his position. We'd become so finely attuned.

So much that I could tell something was off from the arrangement of his parts as he stood outside to meet me as I got to school. I couldn't tell if there was too much motion or too little in him as I walked toward him standing, like he was a spider, and I couldn't tell whether or not he was about to make a move or if he had one planned or if he was just waiting. I couldn't tell if it was my vision failing or my reason but one way or the other, I needed it resolved, because without him there wasn't anyone left to love me.

Brian let me walk all the way up to him before he started to turn like we were both supposed to. He said hello but on the move, like it was important to get something over with, too important to acknowledge me proper in a way that took time. I followed him through the double doors and felt like he was doing this, this little walk he had us on, to lead us both to something final. The more he weaved through the other people and expected me to do the same, bump right, go left, keep up, don't lose him; other people are just something that we move between, stuck so much to their places that there wasn't any point to commingling or working in some way together, obstacles to our focal point that weren't worth the recognition of looking up, and walking this way I soon began to wonder if that's what happened to me as well. What happened to my recognition. What end would this walk have? In no other hundred metres had I ever gone through as many possible futures, and I thought that this must be what death row felt like, except we were moving so fast and they so slow, and if the people we were weaving around weren't better cognizant that at the end there's only ends and deaths and maybe their being in the way was only a result of that cognition. Is the only thing that separates me and Brian from the rest of humanity that we run toward death? If I'd had a second to think about it, maybe I'd be one of them too; maybe that was the difference between us. I felt like crying, but knew I wasn't allowed to; crying is for people who have people who might care and after all, we're just walking down a hall.

There isn't much of it left. By now I'd settled into destiny so far that I anticipated we'd walk straight out the set of doors on the other end of the hallway and keep going. Keep going down the hill out back where I smoked, across the athletic fields and between the portable classrooms until we found the river, where we'd keep going. Cross to the other side or stop fighting and go with the current, me clinging to Brian as he still refused to meet my gaze, because he'd doomed us both, decided for us both, that it was time to drown or worse, face whatever waited at the riverbank, where at some point he'd grasp onto an errant branch and pull me to land just to keep going, The motion our new lives.

But that didn't happen, none of it did. In the usual manner, my thoughts moved faster than our bodies and by the time we'd reached our destination, I'd already lived through countless never-lives, all with one thing in common—that I didn't get to choose them. I let Brian lead in all of them and cursed myself for it now, retrospectively. I should have grabbed him, made him face me, and I still could, if only he hadn't done it himself.

We were stopped at the corner outside of the music hall, where they kept the instruments and taught courses in media in the afternoons, away but only slightly from the mass of drones playing at human lives, and I realized I'd not been looking at Brian this whole time but at nothing, the nothing one sees when we're too focused on the abstract to register anything appearing to the senses. But when I finally looked at him, I saw that the determination that I'd felt in our death march thus far wasn't coming from a place of authority but from a desperation that he get done something he didn't want to do. That he had something someone needed him to make happen and, while he maybe didn't feel right about it, the thing had to be done, and so it would be. That thing was just to bring me here to—what? And then I felt it. A force more powerful than Brian's or perhaps equal, but eclipsing his pull on me, which I felt at once as a shift in physical forces as well as an intellectual intuition of the fact that if Brian hadn't meant to do something, that there was something more powerful that meant him to, and all at once whatever that thing was, replaced him in my hierarchy of desires, things toward which to be.

And there he was as flesh.

Brian's body opened up as if to accept another being into its space and thus my gaze too shifted to the right where I saw a boy standing, tall but not tall enough to be strange. Black hair with blue eyes, gaunt but not sallow, pale but not sickly, close to the edge of where human proportionality could stretch and remain recognizably human, but safe within that confine. He was definitely a boy, not a monster or a demon or anything otherworldly that one sees in bathroom mirrors late at night. He was wearing white and black and so I checked to make sure his flesh and eyes still had colour in them, that he wasn't somehow drawn upon this reality in a chalk or charcoal deception, something that looked human but wasn't. The colours were still there but even so, even with the proportions figured out, the definite facial features that took on a pleasant countenance, the blue eyes that fixated on me as I made my examinations—even with all of that in place, there was something of the uncanny in the air about him. The shine on his shoes was too white to reflect the fluorescents above. The distance between his eyes and mine was too much to feel this sort of connection. Sensation at a distance. Though Brian kept his body in between ours and we never had the opportunity to touch, already I was ensconced in him and I thought maybe, this is what Brian knew would happen, what he didn't want to happen, what he'd even so made happen, all before 8:45. Brian turned to me and said, "This is Vincent," while Vincent smiled like he'd just accomplished something and in doing so let me go a little, let me think of him a little as one person in the world again, let me have that world back I'd just lost and would give up again to have him. Took something back away from me so that I'd want it again, and I did. I fucking did.

With Vincent, the universe got bigger, and I became a smaller part of it.

11

Sometimes I think about that girl who came over for my eighth birthday party and by over, I don't mean over here, I mean my aunt's place out of town, where she had an above-ground pool. I thought that that was pretty good, and it was nice of her to let us use it for my party and so did most everyone else except this one girl. She got out of the car and looked around and when she saw the pool just sitting there on top of the grass, she started crying, because that's not what she thought pools looked like. She tried to get out of it, said she forgot her bathing suit and when I offered to lend her one, just started crying more. We had to call her parents back, which took a while because we had to wait for them to drive home first to pick up the phone. I sat on the front lawn with her and apologized and apologized, for I don't know what. Being this way, I guess.

12

Everything Brian told me about Vincent was a lie or at least, it couldn't have been true. It couldn't have been true that he'd just moved here from a smaller town barely forty minutes away. It can't have been true that he too had a family, that somehow his mother had impinged upon Brian's mother, because of some elective affiliation from the past that she'd called upon to make sure that when her son got to school, someone would have to show him around. It would go how these things always went—that the person intended to be the connection to the new environment becomes something of a hindrance and then is politely ignored, as the new person finds their own environment in which to exist. But I couldn't imagine anywhere else that Vincent might fit in except with us, with Brian, with me.

If it were true that he'd come from not so far away, it would support the supposed affiliation between their mothers. Because they were both from comfortable families, and people who grew up comfortably don't have the same urge to get as far away from their homes as possible. Because they'd have the sort of relationship that would allow for the any time calling in of favours, even when those favours may not be repaid, especially when they might not be, because both parties could afford to bank one— just in case. I thought of my own family and how none of them spoke to us, to me, any longer. How when there's nothing to get from someone, those social bonds cease.

I didn't know yet what there was to love about Vincent, except that my body responded to him in a way that indicated there must be something. Something significant. It felt like I had gotten my period and during my first class, I stuck my fingers under my dress and looked for stains, to make sure that when I stood up there wouldn't be a pool of blood underneath me. But the timing was off and anywhere, there was nothing there. I saw a girl across the room look at me, horrified, but then again, that's what she always did.

At lunch hour, Vincent joined us in the hallway, sat up in a row against the lockers. I knew that if I sat with my knees up to brace myself that people walking by could see up my skirt. Brian made sure I knew that and when he told me, he'd seemed a bit upset about it, like I should have known, taken more care, figured out what the world looked like from someone else's point of view and what they saw and thought of me besides, like it was my responsibility to know this. I couldn't sit with my legs crossed either, for much the same sort of reason. So I leaned against Brian with my knees bent to the other side, which made my pelvis hurt but at least wouldn't get me in trouble. Vincent and Brian talked about movies and music, and Brian was disappointed to find that he couldn't find anything to mention that Vincent hadn't heard of, didn't already know. Vincent hadn't brought anything to eat, so I used it as an excuse to change positions, sit in the front of both of them, share a Ziploc bag of crackers I'd brought from home. Vincent seemed to appreciate how the little baggie flew in the face of any conventional definition of what a lunch might consist of, and every time he took some, looked me in the eye and laughed a little, if not out loud, then definitely in his eyes.

In his eyes I could see everything I was meant to be and do.

At one point Brian had to get up, to see someone about something, some guy he'd written an essay for, about, or otherwise had dealings with. The feeling that went through me as he stood up to leave me alone with Vincent, if only for a moment, felt like cocaine after a hard hangover. For a moment I was sad for Brian, who knew my body so well that he must have been able to feel it, sad for myself for having lost a little of him, and only since this morning, like having someone die, but they're only dead to me. No, I thought, that's a little much. It's not that he meant nothing to me or even that I didn't love him, but I also felt that whatever I'd do now, whatever Vincent had come here for, it was all already set in motion, and I knew I'd do whatever I could to make it happen.

When Brian was about twenty feet away, I shifted positions, crossed my legs in front of Vincent and tucked my dress between them, let my hand linger a little and saw no sign Vincent was horrified. Instead, and as if to confirm what I'd been feeling for only hours now, that my life was on a new trajectory, a new course with different players and with a definite though yet unknown end, Vincent leaned forward and waited for me to do the same, so close to me that from either side, no one would have been able to tell if he were speaking or just looking, smiling or just staring, and no one would be able to hear him say to me, "Hey," in a low tone of voice that, like earlier today, felt like it was touching me across the space between us, "I'm glad I found you," just to lean back and sever the connection, though something had just begun.

13

You might see behind your glasses
What it is that hasn't been
But everything will have its turn
Nothing leaves here without sin

Unfortunately, it isn't true that once one's fate has been decided, once it is all set in motion, when all that will be has become inevitable, that we don't still have to go to work. But Christie would still want money from me at the end of the month, plus all the other money going out besides. Cheryl couldn't do without me on a weekend, anyway. If the divinities wanted it so, they could have gotten me out of work, I reasoned, so there must be a reason I'm here. Some bigger reason than to butter rolls and scrub cooked potatoes out of the holes in the colander, because Cheryl complained that Jackson never did it right. So at the end of the night, she'd tell him he was done, go home, and let me clean up after his having cleaned up, which didn't cost her much at my rate.

What it comes down to is that even if I was just cutting radishes, even if nothing I did had any significance whatsoever, even if it all would be forgotten tomorrow and it would be, still someone was depending on me to do it, someone who might suffer if I didn't.

It was hell, though, going through the motions when now that my fate was sealed all I wanted to do was advance the situation. It's the devil's trick that things take time and that we all have to live through it. I felt Vincent now, stronger than ever, and you'd think that it'd be nice to always have somebody, but it wasn't in that kind of way. Kind of like it was with my mother, the more he cares about you, the more it hurts. I didn't want to think that he only came when she left me, but things did seem to line up like that. Maybe the main thing about a mother is that they're supposed to keep the devil away. Not let him in. Not let him in and let him have you. Not let him in and let him have you and leave him in charge.

I bussed tables and made sure that the recycling ended up in the recycling. Cheryl said there was a complaint that we were putting soda cans in the trash. But everyone here knew as well as I did that there was only one option when they came to take the trash away, and that was the dumpsters down near the lagoon where my mom's stuff continued to go. There wasn't one for cans and one for paper, one for clothes for the needy, one for ashes from the woodstove. There was just one kind, and everything went in it but before that, I guess I'd separate it out, if it made that person happy.

I boiled pasta and cut up celery. We'd put Russian dressing on it and call it pasta salad. There was only one order that needed it, and that was the salad plate. Potato salad, pasta salad, cheese and ham and coleslaw. People who liked cold food would order it, and Molly said it was for people who worked the fields all day and needed something to cool off, and I didn't think she knew what she was talking about. But she knew about the devil.

"He's here today; I can feel him," Molly said.

Cheryl told me that it was part of her mental illness.

Thing was, it didn't matter if the plates kept going out. You don't get to be ill when people are depending on you and besides that, if it didn't stop you from doing what you're meant to be doing it was like it wasn't there at all.

I just knew that ever since Vincent showed up, I couldn't live through a moment, even though I could. I could wipe the counters, bring out checks, count tips, grill sandwiches and make sure there was coffee on; there's always coffee on but at no time I wasn't worried what Vincent and Brian are up to and that I wasn't with them. I held onto that moment from when Vincent came, when Brian left us alone, and I told myself that it would happen again, if only there was some moment again, when there wasn't someone else and something else to stop it. But Brian and Vincent spent all their time together, and it was like it hadn't happened even though I knew it did. Ever since that day he came, it was like he was just some boy, some boy who came to live here and who made a friend and spent all their time with them, and sometimes their girlfriend came along and that was me.

But it wasn't like that, was it. I wasn't an appendage. Whenever we were all together, there was something to it, something more than what Brian and I had before. But I worried for the same reason I didn't—because of that moment in the hallway when my fate was sealed. How many moments had gone by that I wasn't there for? It wasn't fair, but maybe it was necessary. Things take time. Things take time to develop, and maybe that's all that was going on, but it sure seemed like Vincent had forgotten about me and maybe so did Brian. Except he made sure we still fucked. He liked to pick me up and fuck me at the trailer before we'd leave to go get Vincent. He said I smelled differently, and he liked it. He wanted Vincent to know I'd been recently fucked, like it made him somehow cooler.

If I'd had fifteen seconds with Vincent alone, the world might have exploded.

Something's not ready yet, my devil told me, and he was never wrong.

Only vague.

On the other hand, I looked around at all the forgotten people and wondered how easy it'd be to forget me too. Moment to moment. All at once. It only took a second. It's the forgotten ones that have to live through it. All the moments after. The disgrace of it.

I had to have faith in the devil, or else I'd be fucked.

I was walking back from table six with dirty plates when Molly leaned over and whispered, "If it weren't for you...." But the sentence didn't have an ending yet, because the thing that wouldn't be if not for me still hadn't happened.

14

It'd been three weeks since I met Vincent, and I was starting to think that nothing had changed. It couldn't be true,
though. Why do my thoughts tend toward the impossible?
Because of how little changes in the actual expressions
of the will of divinities. Because of how trivial it is to see
power played out in the physical realm. Because of all the
things that could change, none of them supersede the lower level flesh prisons to which we're all currently confined.

But I, I had a hint of the divine.

When Brian differentiated between humans and people, the distinction wasn't so grand as what I now envisioned. He was thinking *too small*. He wasn't thinking of
a beyond, transcending what was and could be. I was
wrong too, thinking that the difference might be one of
classes or activities or just some people better than others;
the fact of the matter is that there are people with a hint of
the other side and, while I didn't know how to get there
just yet, it was definitely there, and it took me.

I felt a summons.

The worst thing about the devil is he works in implications.

And he's funny.

I couldn't tell if it was another joke he was playing on me or if this time, the feeling was right, but I knew I'd act anyway or wouldn't have to.

Something's going to happen.

Something's going to happen tonight.

The mundanity of the event is one of his jokes, too. Like we're going to alter the course of existence on earth and it's going to happen at some teenager's birthday party.

We're all invited. Vincent and Brian had got in with some crowd at school and now we're all integrated. They put up with me, even though I was strange, but I'm only strange because I recognize the impermanence of all they have created. There's no social bond that isn't subject to condition, no tether to the other that's going to persist beyond material circumstances. I looked around at these people and thought of where they'd all be once the bonds dissolved, when one of them moved, someone died, someone said the wrong thing, how temporary it all was and how little point there was in becoming attached. And on the other end of the matter is that there was nothing to attach to, like putting stickers on Vaseline. I had no attraction to them and they couldn't tell what that was, because I'm supposed to be tending toward associations by nature, not by force.

At best I'd be a thing that could easily be ignored, and that depended on me doing my best to be that thing. Even so, there was Brian, and there was Vincent. What the fuck did they see in these people? Before roping me along, Brian tried to convince me that they weren't so bad, that somehow, in some way, they'd actually met his usually impossible standards of what constituted a good human—and all of them? No. And there was this one girl.

I knew he thought that she was pretty, and I let him think it, because what else is there to do? You try to change people's thoughts, and they hold on to them tighter, make it manifest.

The devil knew that thoughts became realities at some point.

Brian had been fucking me mechanically for a week. Like he used to say little things and touch me in ways that made me think I was there too, but instead, he'd almost started ignoring me, except for the contact that was required. It made me think of how he'd once described his forays into masturbation and how at first, he didn't think of anyone or anything at all. At first, he said, it was entirely about the physical sensation, and I wondered if we were now fucking in that framework or if it was just a bad week.

But I knew there was no such thing as an endless point in time. All things are a trajectory and you're either on it or not—depending on how much you want to suffer.

And of course it was me too, because of Vincent. But at this point, I couldn't envision how exactly that might play out and so hadn't thought to change things with Brian. Even so, a lull in our connection might be me implicitly detaching from the situation, to allow for new attachments.

Meanwhile, Vincent continued to pretend he was a normal boy.

He was coming to this girl's birthday party, the one Brian thought was pretty. I wondered if I'd see his mom drop him off at the door, see evidence of his integration into some unbefitting social structure. See him promise to be home at a certain time or maybe even arrange a later pickup. All these images served to humanize him but not in a good way, not in a way that made me think that the current trajectories of existence might meet their satisfactory end. Thank goodness none of that came to pass.

When Brian came to get me from the trailer, Vincent was already in the car.

And there was a smell to him.

At the other end of the ride was a suburban house you could distinguish from the others on the street only by the numbers. Someone had put up a banner on the front porch with one step up that said, "Happy Birthday Bridget", and it reminded me of the streamers I'd got to put up once at the bar when my mom brought me in too early in the day. They were setting up for Halloween night and they told her that she shouldn't have me in there, but it wasn't after 9 or anything which is when they had to kick out all the minors, so they said I could help out putting up the streamers. I opened package after package, twisting one colour inside another and adding up how much it cost them to do it that way, two colours in one, instead of just the one colour. I must have gone through thirty dollars of streamers that day, and there was a peculiar joy in it, in throwing money away on colours and in getting to do that when I wouldn't have got to at home. Bridget's banner must have cost a lot more than that, every letter a different colour and metallic, with little metal gromets holding each one to the next.

She was turning sixteen, and I knew why Brian thought she was pretty. Her big eyes and cute, slumped over frame that made you want to pick her up and carry her off somewhere safe. I might have done it myself. It wasn't her fault for being who she was; it was Brian's fault—for what? For getting me to fuck him, I imagined, just so that every year from now on he could find someone a year younger and do it again, not because they were younger, but because he wanted to seem more knowledgeable, more experienced, though I knew it didn't seem like him. And besides, I didn't want to have to think about it when I had my own designs on Vincent.

That was different.

The constitution of reality depends on it.

I couldn't think about what once was. But I knew that whatever happened, if it happened, wouldn't stop me from thinking of Brian as mine.

Of course I loved him.

Of course I loved him AND.

Balloons floated to the ceiling inside Bridget's house. Her parents promised to stay upstairs. We had the main floor and the basement. Snacks removed from packages and poured into serving dishes. A cake someone had bought, with words written on it, even though that cost extra. Nobody else seemed to notice, and for that, I felt alone. What was I doing here, anyway? What were these people to me? They were someones to Brian, but what was he to me? Someone who couldn't possibly get it, no matter how many times he fucked me in my trailer without blinking, the lyrics to Gimme Danger playing havoc with my concept of whether or not, by the time he was done, I should have died already. Maybe it was constantly expected and just yet another thing on which I'd failed to come through. Maybe that's what was so pretty about

Bridget. She had banners and five extra dollars for the icing that wrote letters and when someone expected her to die, she fucking would.

Come now, the devil told me, not in so many words. A feeling of having thought too far.

I found a spot on the lower level of the house and waited it out. Let Brian go talk to strangers. Said no when I was offered food, drinks. I didn't want them to think I lived that way, that I needed or wanted anything. I'm a self-contained end of desire in itself, and I have no requirements. On the walls and on the furniture, pictures of Bridget and a boy the same age. I wondered why that boy wasn't here.

Vincent for the most part followed Brian. He accepted what was offered and I thought, perhaps, that's what I should have done too, become inconspicuous by becoming the average of whatever people existed nearby. It seemed to work well for him.

Bridget opened gifts, but I hadn't thought to bring her anything. As a girl of good breeding, she didn't mention it. The fact that she didn't only widened the gap between our existences. If she could have been just a little oblivious to the proper ways to behave, we might have gotten along, become friends, run off together and left Brian behind. *But what about Vincent?*

Standing in the corner, pretending not to notice how far out of my element I've gone. I had a vision of Vincent and Brian, on all the nights I'd worked, attending events just like this one, letting them become habitual, talking to the people there with ease, getting to know their mundane thoughts, thinking perhaps that because these people were the ones nearby, that their opinions on things were important, that someday they might become helpful, that of all the people in the world with whom to associate, these ones seemed most beneficial, or at least fine, when it seemed obvious to me that these instantaneous interactions had nothing of the divine in them, and that by intermingling amongst themselves, a thorny web would form in the intricate networks undergirding this reality that would bind them to physicality and each other, while I observed from the beyond.

If this is all there is, I thought, I don't want anything to do with it. The thought, instead of making me feel superior, emphasized my alienation from the only world I knew or could know. In the height of my despair, I saw Vincent looking at me, and I remembered for a moment the feeling of having a purpose, something to live for, someone to be for.

"Why don't you get a drink, talk to someone?" he asked me, like he was one of them. And I knew in that moment that I couldn't explain what I'd been thinking, in the moments or weeks before he'd sat down next to me. I couldn't explain how the heat of his side against mine made me feel like I should want to be someone I wasn't, just because he asked. I couldn't answer the question directly in any way that provided a reason, so instead I chose to carry on the interaction by thwarting the question, starting again, and I asked him.

"Vincent?" Like he hadn't spoken yet.

"Mmhmmmmmm?" He responded like he thought I was going somewhere.

"Do you like it here?"

I could have meant this birthday party; I could have meant this town; I also meant this plane of existence, and I wanted to know the answer, so that I could decide myself.

He sat silent for a moment, and I worried that he'd do what I had done just seconds before, change the topic, not answer, deny the inquiry. But instead he thought about it, and he said: "This is where we are, and it shouldn't be any different."

I felt reassured by that, by the fact that he'd used *we* to refer to the both of us, that he thought to include me in the space where he was, and because he seemed certain enough that this was how things were supposed to go. But I wasn't convinced yet, so I asked again.

"Are you sure?"

And the way he smiled, like he knew something I didn't, made it all all right, for the moment.

Maybe I was wrong about Brian too, the way he looked at Bridget like a human just meant he was polite, that he was generally considerate of people, and that maybe these weren't faults. He spent most of the night whispering to Vincent, and I could even see them looking in my direction every now and again, with a look in Brian's eyes that was all and only affectionate. He can't have meant any harm in bringing me here. There wasn't any harm to be done in a place like this. Maybe that's why they were all so comfortable.

I got up and helped myself to a beverage, leaned against a wall, made small talk with some people nearby, told Bridget she had a nice house without adding that she'd been born into it and had nothing to do with its quality. I wished her a happy birthday, and I talked to some other people about courses we were in, who was teaching them, what we'd heard about them, how Mr. Johnson sometimes smoked weed out back behind the greenhouse with the art teachers, that while you wouldn't think that art teachers and botanists would get along so well, they just had to find something in common. They forgave me my first hour of silence, because it was easier to, and you can always rely on people to want to have the most pleasant experience they can, as long as they're not me.

Vincent looked at me approvingly, and I knew that I'd done well. Brian seemed happy that I'd pleased Vincent, which struck me as strange but all together positive. I kept telling myself that these were hours to get through, that time had to pass, that something had to happen, and that one way or another, I'd be involved in it.

And I knew that I'd done the right thing only when, in the depths of the evening, when I'd reached the pinnacle of integration with the microsociety just formed by those who could attend versus not attend, as we formed these bonds forever, I saw Vincent go into the bathroom after Brian. I saw Brian try to shut the door and Vincent stop it. I saw Brian try to pull Vincent forward as he moved backward, to find another way that nobody could see. I saw that in defiance, Vincent pulled Brian's head into the four-inch band of light that shone from inside to outside. I saw Vincent looking at me straight through Brian. I saw Brian close his eyes as Vincent kissed him on the mouth. I saw Vincent; I saw Brian; and I saw the devil; and I knew what he had done and that this, all of this, was part of it.

15

When it was time to leave, I had Brian go to my place first, and I knew that when he looked at Vincent for approval, there it'd be. I knew that when he stopped the car, I'd get out and so would Vincent, and then he'd have to turn it off and come in too. I knew that when I unlocked the door, I could expect them both to go in. I knew that they might notice the reduction of material things inside, and that while they might wonder at the change, they wouldn't say anything about it.

I had enough furniture for myself, and a few things.

I knew that I'd touch Brian first, to let him know everything was all right. He was playing a role he didn't yet understand, and he hadn't done anything wrong. I knew that when his lips relaxed, I'd bite him on the neck, which always got his dick hard. I knew that after I confirmed it with my hand, I'd feel Vincent behind me, putting his hands up and down my sides and Brian's, a seamless third party. The warmth on both sides of my body from others made a heat run through me that I'd never felt when sex was limited to just one person, who could only warm me from one side at a time, leaving the other side cold and unloved.

I pushed Brian toward the bed, and Vincent followed. I let Vincent sit on the floor and watch as I carried through the motions with Brian that we'd done so many times before. I noticed how his responses were more enthusiastic, how he seemed more sensitive to touch, and how while he tried to pretend Vincent wasn't there, he was and Brian knew it. He was only pretending for show, some misguided idea of doing it for my sake. I knew that in this moment I would have to make Brian feel loved, and that I could, and how even though I was doing it for someone else, that wouldn't diminish it. As I laid Brian down and removed his clothes, I saw Vincent mimicking the motions, taking his own clothes off to sit back down. As I got on top of Brian and started to move up and down, I saw him keeping pace with me with his hands. There was something aggressive in the way he masturbated, not toward himself but as an affront to some unknown resistance, against which we were all fighting by increasing sensations beyond the ones felt by the living.

I held Brian's face in my hands, and I leaned in over him, breathing the same air as he did while curving my back and allowing the air to escape the vacuum between our torsos, a circulatory system of hot and cold, warm and dry. I turned his face to Vincent and let him see it was all right, there was nothing to be worried about here. Finally, I leaned back and reached for his balls, holding them and rubbing the hard spot just behind, and as he orgasmed into me, I covered his mouth and retained the sounds about to burst forth, thinking that the energy contained should redirect itself into my uterus.

With Brian finished, I let him breathe a little before I stood up, and so did Vincent. I bent over where Brian lay on the bed and kissed him, while Vincent took up a place behind me. As Vincent slid his dick into me, I could feel the semen Brian had left in me start to warm, to thicken. As Vincent held on to me, he too leaned over and kissed Brian laying on the bed, to let him know it was all right. Not only was Vincent's cock warmer than Brian's, it felt like it was getting bigger every time he pulled it out and pushed it back in, until I thought that maybe this time my body would reject it, he wouldn't be able to push through, my organs wouldn't readjust themselves around this massive cock that threatened every one of us.

I remember that as he orgasmed, I couldn't see anything at all, but I was thinking of the devil in the ceiling stain above us.

I remember thinking that Vincent's body was unnatural, that it wasn't constrained by the same physical limitations as the rest of them, and I wondered if Brian felt that too, when he had fucked him, which I now assumed he had.

I could feel his too-hot semen intermingling with Brian's. I could feel the helixes of their DNA separate and recombine. I could feel a new organism being created. I could feel its thoughts and intentions, but I couldn't yet make them out in words. I knew that they weren't good. I knew that the thing we'd just made was nothing other than the devil I'd always known existed near me, and I knew that when the formation was complete, that what we'd done was give the devil a body, that it was mine, no longer mine, ours, our body, mine and the devil's and in a different way Brian's and Vincent's, though neither of them could have accomplished alone what we'd done just now together. I knew that whatever I was before, I was more of it now, and that Vincent had everything to do with it, that this was the point in time to which all other points in time had pointed, that this was what had to happen. I felt the other being crystallize along my nervous system, a vibration in my heart, an electricity in my brain, and a sensation unknown to humanity in my fingertips.

I saw everything clearly and distinctly, for the first time.

I saw Vincent put his finger to his lips, and I felt my teeth get harder.

We're not done.

Part Three

16

EXISTENCE IS THE THIRD INTEGRAL.

VOLUMINOUS PRESENCE.

STRUCTURE AND PURPOSE.

EARTHLY ARE THE MATERIAL THINGS.

DIVINE IS THEIR ARRANGEMENT.

EVIL IS ITS NEGATION.

TEETH THAT TEAR FOR PAIN.

FIRES THAT LIVE TO BURN.

I AM THE SPACE BETWEEN RATIONAL THOUGHTS THAT LETS
LOOSE THE HEART'S VENGEANCE.

WHAT KILLS WHAT WANTS TO LIVE.

THE IMBALANCE OF THE ELEMENTS.

THE INTENSITY OF THE NOTE THAT MAKES IT HARD TO HEAR.

THE SENTIMENT IT CAUSES.

I AM EVERY MEMORY YOU WISH YOU'D FORGOTTEN.

ITS RISING.

EVERY INSTANCE OF TOO MUCH AND OF TOO LITTLE.

WHAT HAPPENS WHEN IT GOES WRONG.

THIS BODY DOESN'T HAVE THE SORT OF HAND IT TAKES TO HOLD ME.

ITS HUMORS DON'T COMBINE IN ALL MY WAYS.

HOWEVER LONG IT TAKES I WILL ABIDE THE LAWS IT'S BROUGHT ME.

DEATH AND LIFE AND DEATH AGAIN.

THE LOGIC TOO DARK TO NAME.

When I woke up in the morning, I was alone. I remembered everything I had done. But I was different.

There was a lack.

An atmospheric anxiety was missing from the perception of my body. The way it had always been, the body had been a tether. No matter how delicate my sensibilities, how nuanced my thoughts, there it had been, demanding rest, demanding sustenance, exerting a pain if I had the gall to expose it to a temperature that wasn't exactly adequate to its preferred form of functioning. Now, there'd been a shift in the dynamic. It was less like it controlled me, and more like it relied on me for its needs.

But I could deny it.

And if I did, it would still enact its duties, under threat of a greater force. If I fed it, kept it safe, allowed it rest, it would be a favour, repaid with interest. It took its proper place of subjugation in relation to the intellect that ruled it. Like a possession, it would do whatever I desired.

And if I tired of it, it would be destroyed.

The burden of proof on my body to convince me of its usefulness.

My house, too—the trailer. I didn't feel its confines as strongly as I once had. I couldn't sense the precarity in the way the walls held together, holding the heat inside, my existence's dependence on its shoddily maintained infrastructure. I felt as if, were the walls to fall down around me right now, there I'd stand among the debris, among the carnage, and I would rule it as I would any other material form.

So slight is the difference between structure and destruction, health and decay, life and death.

I thought of feelings I'd once had and how they'd become unworthy of me.

The sentimentality I'd felt for mother's things.

The last of it was what was inside the closet and the furniture. I'd managed to contain it to containers, at least. I could argue that the last of it was things she hadn't touched for years, things behind the other things, inaccessible for the things that had piled up around them, preventing her from opening the doors or the drawers of the cupboards. The things inside have waited all this time for their own sort of freedom. But soon they would have to go.

I had to make more room for myself to exist in.

Gone was my fear that time would proceed without my input.

On my way to the bathroom, I stubbed my toe on the short step up from my bedroom to the kitchen, and I laughed. I laughed because it hurt, and I laughed because that no longer mattered. I knew how many minutes it would take to modify my flesh form into the expected state of readiness. I knew I wouldn't miss the bus.

I knew that if I did, that wouldn't matter either.

Gone was the neurotic speculation of what Brian was doing at this very moment, what he was thinking of without me, whether he still cared.

I knew that when I arrived, he would be there.

And so would Vincent.

What was he?

I washed my skin and hair, pinching it in places. I wanted it to know that I could tear it off if I so chose. I took some skin from my abdomen, to the right of my navel, and I held it between my thumb and index finger. I pushed the nail of my thumb into it, feeling its resistance and watching its colour turn. I knew that if I put a hole in it, it would do its best to repair. It was so much more attached to its wholeness than I was.

Something to use against it, like anything anyone cares about.

I dried my hair and thought that it looked pretty, blonde and flowing to my shoulders. I put on a red lipstick and thought of Marilyn Monroe, her cunt mouth. And now mine. Another symbol of control. I smiled and, when I saw my teeth in the mirror, smiled larger, until my face was all teeth and lip. I leaned my head back to make the illusion appear in the mirror of my mouth engulfing the rest of my face, my brows, my eyes, receding into darkness as the mouth expanded farther than flesh would allow.

Then I snapped my jaw shut.

I had to go to school.

I left my coffee cup in the sink and bundled up. It was supposed to be cold. I was supposed to worry about that. As I laced up my boots, I felt the same draught coming in through the doorframe where the door had warped away from the corners. That draught had kept me up at night and blew snow onto my face while I was sleeping. Now the wind felt like it was meant for me, like the movement of the air solidified my relationship to this body by providing constant proof that I could feel what it felt.

It wasn't cold; it was life.

I shut off the propane, so it wouldn't kick in later when it got cold.

I locked the door.

Walking one kilometre from the trailer door to where the bus stopped, I passed by other trailers, the shed where they kept the mailboxes where once I'd sat through the night, left outside by my mother, who'd failed to return that evening with the only set of keys. I didn't have the guts to break a window. I thought about breaking one now to make up for it. But not mine. Children came out of some doors, aiming to catch the same bus I would. I saw the woman who'd accused me of poisoning her at the restaurant. Old potato salad, she'd said. Luckily she wasn't anyone worth listening to. "It was probably something in her godforsaken house," Cheryl had said when she complained. The kids always came out smelling. I pictured them in there, skin rotting in the fabric of the furniture, fluids seeping from them and staining the floors, everything always wet, never drying despite the best efforts of the air, because of the moistness of their breath and its own stench.

I saw Edward in the window, and he gave me a little wave.

Poor Edward.

I don't know why my mother wouldn't just give in and love Edward. He was constantly pining for her. He sat at home on disability, which was more than she could do. (Her disability claims were denied; she had to sit at home without it.) He would have been better for her than any of the losers that she did fuck.

I think that she was keeping Edward on reserve, as proof that she could always have somebody when the others didn't work out. And she died with Edward in her savings account. She didn't want to think that she was the sort of woman who would date a man who lived in a trailer park. She thought she could do better than herself for herself.

She thought that if she made someone with money love her a little, she wouldn't have to be this person anymore. But they knew, they knew they could have what they wanted from her and not give her anything, after all, nobody else had, and everyone so far had gotten away with it. So the plan didn't work. The plan to live small and make someone feel bad for her *didn't work*. Not with Leonard, not with John, not with Uriah or Scott or the other Scott or the other John or any of the other anyone-but-Edwards she would go out with and not come home with, another message on the answering machine telling me to keep the fire going, the tone in her voice trying to sound concerned because, I could tell, she wanted them to think she cared. Little reminders of all the things she'd never helped me do.

All it meant was that I'd get the bathroom in the morning, that I wouldn't have to worry about someone else in the way for a while.

She didn't appreciate that if she'd only dated Edward, she'd not have gotten *hurt* so badly. She didn't count that as a valuable form of currency, but god damn it, she should have. She shouldn't have loved all the people she'd loved, and she should have loved ones she didn't.

Like Edward.

Like me.

Edward's face in the window so sad, like he'd just remembered he'd have to live through the rest of his life alone. He used to be happy to see me.

I got on the bus and leaned my face against the window, feeling the cold of it.

Edward should have gotten more of her than he did, I thought.

At the transfer station, I switched buses to the one going to the high school, while the small children made their way to their own buses. I was glad to be rid of them, because the switchover meant that by the time I got to school, nobody would have to know where I'd come from. Where I'd come from, I was too old for school by now; the rest of the people my age had dropped out. Finishing my senior year was a sign of immaturity, like I didn't know yet what my fate was or didn't know enough to accept it.

None of this matters, I thought.

What mattered was that when I got off this bus, I would enter the school doors, walk fifty feet to the left, past the office, turn right, turn right again at the corner, and then thirty feet down the hall, I'd find Brian and Vincent waiting.

And someone else with them?

No, Bridget was just walking past when I made my second right. When she saw me, she kept her head down, as if out of deference. It was like she knew she wasn't allowed to be there when I arrived. But who'd told her that? For a moment it was like yesterday and all the days before, when everything was a source of concern and every look meant something of the unknown, when anyone could bring an end to it all while I had my head turned away for an instant. But no. That's not how it is anymore. Now, as Bridget tried to slink by without creating enough wind to ruffle her stick-straight brown hair so that I wouldn't detect her motion and know that she existed, I stopped her. I stopped her moving with a look and the authority that came from being one year older, taller, prettier, more colourful and more bold. Because from now on nothing was going to happen that I didn't have a part in, so I told her: "Hey. Come back and sit with us at lunch."

And that's when it started between us. The look she gave me, of gratitude for having acknowledged her at all, for not resenting her for existing near to the boys I thought were mine; it might have been the first time she made eye contact with me, and when she did, she'd seen a well of good intent, a welcoming gaze, a genuine interest, all the things you'd hope to see in the eyes of a new friend.

Fucking weakass cunt.

"Sure," she said and gleamed.

I didn't have her yet, but it was a start.

I nodded and said, "Great, see you then," before continuing down the hall, with a little wave behind me to let her know I'd meant it. All of this in view of Brian, who couldn't have known what to think or how to react and so said nothing. As I approached, I grabbed his right hand with my left and kissed him on the mouth, to let him know where we stood. While his eyes were closed, I opened mine and looked at Vincent behind him, leaning against a locker, smug as he'd ever been, but so was I. I put my right hand on his chest and felt his heartbeat—a slow bass rhythm, like his blood was thicker than the rest of ours. But it still circulated in a human body.

And isn't that what counts.

Behind Brian, I saw the vice principal who'd brought him to her office for this.

"I'm so sorry!" I told her as she advanced on us. "I'm so sorry, Mrs. Finnigan!" I said as she kept coming.

"I'm so sorry you have no one, Mrs. Finnigan!" I yelled even as she came nearer. "I'm sorry Mr. Finnigan died, but you don't need to take it out on me!" I screamed as she stopped. I started walking toward her, with the aim of going past, but first I faked a cough. "Cancer, was it?!" I coughed and coughed. "Oh honey, you'd better get that checked out!" I said as I moved around her, toward my classroom. "How hard would that have been to say?" I knew from experience that from her perspective, the few people around would seem like thousands; I could hear her ego deflating as the tears started in her eyes, see that if she said anything back to me, they'd fall with the movement of her mouth. I saw her decide to stay silent, to contain the damage to this hallway and hope that I hadn't just broken the air of authority she had to maintain for the sake of her job, her means of income as a widow. I saw her eyes decide not to engage with me, not now, and perhaps not ever again, and it made me feel powerful, like I'd accomplished something important, come out from under something weighty, and that the venom I was spitting worried her, because perhaps we're all like this, all of the students, and I was just the one to open the floodgate. How thin has the ice been on which she's been skating all this time? How bad could it get? What if this was the start of something, at the end of which she'd have no choice but to mind her own business, be polite, and collect a paycheque.

Fucking Mrs. Finnigan. What kind of person decides that what they want to do with their life is order teenagers around? The kind of person who wants to order adults around but doesn't have the guts or the money or the qualifications. A sad old woman whose power extends to the end of the parking lot. As I kept going, I turned around, walked backwards a couple of steps, smiled and blew a kiss, and I thought that I'd never end up like Mrs. Finnigan, because I wouldn't live to be that old or that sad. While she remained trapped in a body that was trapped in this space, I'd be free.

My early exit from that interaction meant that I had a few minutes to go to the bathroom before class. I felt the millipedes first and then saw them in the toilet when I stood up. I made sure all of them went down in one flush.

17

Bridget came back at noon hour.

The moment I saw her, I felt the confirmation of a power I wasn't yet sure I had, though it was simple enough. The power to tell someone to do things that they'll do. I suppose it was because I'd heard *No* so often in my life. But in my perception of her coming toward me down the hall, as she closed the distance between us, I felt that in addition to the space, there was a tether that I knew she couldn't break.

And I controlled the tension.

It was weird to think that days ago I'd thought of this girl as some kind of threat, when she was mine, my threat. My threat against them.

My new best friend.

Oh, and she was so pretty.

Not like I was pretty, in a way that grabbed attention. She was pretty in a way that wouldn't, and that made boys feel comfortable around her. She was pretty but not alien, not too far out of normal that she wouldn't smile, wouldn't talk to them, wouldn't laugh at what they said.

I pictured her being asked on a lot of study dates, where she would contribute equally to the conversation but never say anything out of the ordinary, no phrases that weren't expected, have no thoughts that weren't reactive. The girl was completely inoffensive but in that, there's a loveliness. Her skin was not made up but sat there, pore-less, stretched over prominent cheekbones which, in a rounded face, made sure she'd never be accused of being striking. Her brown hair had a sheen like it had never met a blowdryer, cut flat across the bottom and tucked behind her ears. She wore no jewelry, but I could see her ears had been pierced at one time. I'd read of Marilyn Monroe once that she preferred not to wear jewelry, so it wouldn't distract from her. I dare say Bridget couldn't wear jewelry, because she'd disappear beneath it.

But bodies are made for purposes, and while mine might have been designed to seduce men, Bridget was made to make them love her.

I could see it now.

At least four inches shorter than I was, her slumped physical form had an unobtrusive charm that made you think she'd spent most of her life unseen. And I knew by now that boys would value the rarity of it—to be the only one to appreciate this unseen loveliness, to tend to it, to, under the guise of protection, ensure no other suitors might approach it, and all of this possible because what they'd actually seen in her at first glance is someone who wouldn't be seen. The purpose of a girl like this is to be torn down enough to be isolated, vulnerable, her mannerisms developed to ward off attack, whereas someone clever might come along and use that to make her love them back.

And that—that—is what I feared Brian was doing when I noticed that he'd noticed her. He was looking for someone easier to be with, nicer to him, compliant, average in every way.

But I would have her first.

And the first thing to do would be to ruin the façade. Make her admit to having secret thoughts and feelings that would make her recognizable, a thing upon which it was impossible to project one's own desires because it already has its own, person with a will and designs by which to achieve it.

Just talk to the poor girl.

I wonder how many people have been uninterested in what she's had to say.

If she's learned not to say it because of them.

Brian and Vincent were already with me at our spot by the lockers, and when Bridget first arrived, she seemed to angle toward Brian, probably the safest one of us. I wondered where she'd got that impression and what sort of relationship they already had that would make her think it. But whatever it was, here we are now, and things are different.

Things are very different.

Brian and Vincent had already gleaned that things, as they were, were very different, and as Bridget approached, their chatter about the thickness of guitar picks versus bass picks resolved, as they too wanted to see what I was up to.

So I intercepted her angle with a wave of my hand and indicated first where she should sit, remembering all the times I had seen for myself the phenomenon that whoever speaks first decides for all. Taking advantage of some weak human tendency not to contradict one another in certain circumstances. And so Bridget sat down next to me. And while the thought occurred to me to apologize for my lack of grace at her party, it occurred to me only as a way of starting the conversation. And I did not want to start the conversation looking weak. And I didn't want to start talking about things that didn't matter, either. People can talk about things that don't matter ad nauseum, and I felt like Bridget would be good at that, but it wouldn't accomplish my goals. So I asked her, once she'd sat down, "Bridget?"

"Yes?" She could have said yeah or mmhmmm or something less formal, but that's just the way she was.

"What role do you have to play here?" I asked her.

"What role?" She said, a request for clarification. Of course I did not expect her to answer the question immediately, but the opportunity to expand on the question would ascertain my current position as leader of the conversation, and put her in a position of trying to find the correct answers, answers that would ensure a harmony amongst all those present, some kind of answer that would determine for us, on an ongoing basis, what Bridget was going to be to our consortium.

"You know that Brian and I are together, and I know he's taken an interest in you." Brian made a scared little face like he didn't think I'd noticed, and I assured him, "That's all fine. The fact that Brian's interested in you doesn't make me jealous, it makes me wonder, what sort of person you are, and what kind of relationship *we* are going to have.

"Because, Bridget, I don't want you to think that we're in any way in competition here. We're not. I have my place.

I want to know what yours is going to be. And what I'd like least of all, is for us to let these boys determine that for us."

Bridget looked back and forth between Brian and Vincent, as if to check that they'd signed off on this. Understandable, since until this point in her life I'd been avoiding her and probably in a way that indicated some deep hatred, jealousy, and resentment. But today, I felt like those sufferings could be set aside in favour of a larger suffering, a suffering yet to be enacted, that would take some time to develop, a suffering that no disdainful look in a high school hallway could comprehend. Brian was still on his guard. He wanted to know where I was going with this, because the longer I talked, the more he tacitly consented, the more of his relationships would be determined for him, going forward. His and mine, his and Bridget's, his and mine and Vincent's... and perhaps some other as yet unforeseen circumstance he could infer from what I was doing.

"Bridget, I think we should be friends and good friends, immediately."

And just the fact that I'd ended my speech on a positive and clear note, after so much dithering, after laying down preconditions for our mutual existence and putting all of that into context, Bridget breathed freely for the first time, a fear dissipating, which indicated to me again that yes, in this relationship, I would be the one in control.

"Yes!" she said, relieved that none of what could have happened had come to pass. "Yes, let's be friends and good friends," she said again, and I took and held her hand, not letting it go as I lowered our hands to her knee.

"I'm so happy that's worked out," Vincent said, smiling like he could see the future.

18

"Go away, devil," is the first thing I heard when I walked into work that night. It was Molly, muttering as she walked from the kitchen past the front door to the table of six in the corner, holding four plates in her hand while Jackson followed behind her with the other two.

The early birds were early.

Cheryl had sent Jordie to pick me up from school in the minivan, they were so early. I was happy to miss the bus, but then there was the 15 minutes of awkwardness in the car as I tried to avoid any kind of conversation. I might have made it easier on myself if I chose to talk myself, about anything, anything but that bench on the lakeside and how that one night about a year ago I'd figured out I didn't belong in yet another place with yet another bunch of people. Something stupid. Something people like to say things about. But I couldn't. At least in all cases time passes and after any given while, everything is over.

It was a quiet night, and I don't mean it wasn't busy. There were people all around, and they were doing all the talking. In the kitchen, there was nothing to say. Cheryl went about the grill and the stovetop, just like she did when I first started. Told me to help out with serving and the cleanup. I didn't want to have to, but I did it. Said the words, made the motions. How's everything? Can I get you a top up? Just the bill then, all right. Well, you have a good night, and we'll see you soon.

Christie was running something down at the rec centre. Games Night. Some bullshit. It started at six, which meant everyone had to be fed by then. Tuckered out and in bed by 8:30. She took the last slot on their schedules, pushed us into second place. But it had been a long time since anything had happened here, and I guess people were happier for it.

I just couldn't imagine the kind of life where Games Night counted as something that happened. At the same time, I couldn't not admit that it was currently changing my life too, the things I did, the way I did them, when and how, to whom. Is this the slippery slope that gets you there, into that kind of life, from where I am?

Am I already living it and just don't know? Like a ghost who doesn't know they're not dead yet?

No, not me. I'd kill myself first, and the thought of it was all relief. There's always a way out.

Cheryl scraped the grill with the putty knife after cooking a round of liver. She wasn't happy, I could tell; it was like before her husband died. Nothing to do with me. Jackson? No, she never took him seriously enough to look that serious about him. Not Jordie, or he wouldn't have got the van. I noticed Molly keeping to the tables, like she'd let me pick up the plates from Cheryl and take them from me on my way out. After a while, I got stuck in the in-between spot that kept the dining room from the kitchen, and that was fine. I kept the coffee pots fresh and put the clean mugs away next to them, took people's cash as they paid their bills and sold candy and cigarettes. I added scoops of ice cream to pieces of apple and cherry pie that Cheryl took out of the box and ran through the microwave for 45 seconds, handed those off to Molly, who'd taken over all the tables by now.

It was like they didn't want to talk to each other.

Even though Molly was laughing, I could tell it wasn't genuine. It's hard to be genuine about someone else going to play games at the rec centre for one thing, but for another thing, she knew she wasn't going. After 6, we'd have dishes as Jackson went off to mop the floors. Molly would smoke and spend an hour refilling whatever needed refilling when all was said and done.

It was all so fucking usual.

I got into my head. It's easy to when you only speak in scripts. People think that if you work here, like it's central, you get to know everyone, but not really. I mean, I know their names and the orders, but I'm not part of the conversation, and I don't get to go to Games Night.

I think that at the end of the day, they'd rather not think I'm a person.

Just like Marilyn. I thought of all the time I had left to live and where Marilyn would have been at my age. It was easier to live through all these moments by imagining others. If I were Marilyn, I'd have twenty years left to live. And that was a lot of time.

And on Friday, I'd have Bridget over. I'd already told her we should "do something this weekend," and the way she looked at me... It was a different sort of adoration than I was used to from Brian. A kind that could go to your head. Marilyn said something like, "If I'm gonna be alone, I wanna be by myself," but what if I didn't have to be?

No, that was a stupid idea.

I'd thought of going to Bridget's house, but I realized I didn't want that. I didn't want her in amongst her things. I wanted her destabilized. I wanted her to feel like I was making someone else of her, someone better. And I was. I'd have her over instead. This place, despite all its sadness, had loneliness at least. I wanted her alone.

With me.

When the place cleared out by 6, I thought that Cheryl might send me home early, finish off the night with Molly, heat up grocery store pizzas for the teenagers who weren't lured in by Games Night, for $2.50 a slice, which wasn't actually a profit. But Cheryl said she needed me. Said that, "Molly's avoiding the kitchen. That's why you've become her runner."

"What's all that about?" I asked her, now that Molly'd gone outside to smoke.

"The chemicals," she said and looked at me.

"The chemicals?" I smiled at her, looking out the screen door at Molly on the picnic table. She was on her second Players Plain.

Cheryl had tears in her eyes, and she tried to say it again, with a straight face, but she couldn't.

"The chemicals!" she said again, her voice rising like she was about to laugh so hard all the neighbours would hear.

I moved around her, dipped my fingers into the bleach bucket and turned around, wiggling them at her from my chest. "The chemicals, Cheryl! The chemicals!"

"No, don't!" she laughed and waved a tea towel around as if to banish me. "Not the chemicals!" she cried.

I lowered my voice, "Yes, the chemicals." And we laughed again, so loud that I knew that if there really were some fight between Cheryl and Molly right now, Molly would know whose side I'd be on.

Cheryl leaned over and talk-whispered at me as I took a cloth from the bleach bucket and wiped down the prep area. "Seriously, though," she said. "You'll have to let her do what she wants for a while. Don't fight her. She's in a state." And while I thought that could have meant a lot of things, I didn't have to wonder very long to figure it all out, because while out the door Molly was lighting her third cigarette after the dinner rush, Cheryl went on: "I'm just glad that I'll be dead by the time that baby grows up."

19

My father isn't home right now.
All who call may leave a message.
None of them will get there.
It's for me again, this time, next time, again.

I knew it would be cold when I got home, because the sweater I'd put on in the morning wasn't doing it on the walk, even with the bodily motion, even with the extra weight of the weekend's newspapers that Cheryl let me have to start fires. I knew that I'd have to keep moving inside until I could get a fire going, get the air heated. I thought it was funny people called this thing a shelter. Once the air got cold enough inside, it felt just like outside. When the show fell, I supposed I'd be happy it wasn't falling directly on me.

I locked the door, but I didn't put the deadbolt on. I'd be going back out again soon. No use putting it on and off again. A waste of good energy, just like running the propane when I could get a fire started instead. I balled up the weekend's Sunshine Girl and put her in the wood-stove. Paper burned sooty, so you don't want too much of it. Soft wood kindling to get it started. Soft wood logs to heat up fast. Hard wood for overnight.

Once the soft wood logs lit, I opened the cupboards that Mom's stuff still inhabited, the "good stuff" hidden behind cupboards and the fronts of drawers, boxes at the back of the closet. I found a box of old family photos and looked at a few before I set the photos aside. My aim was the empty box. It should look like hers, and it would, because it was. It was that soft material meant to recall velvet, but which gathered so much dust to change the colour from burgundy to dull brick. Where my fingers touched it, the dust shifted to reveal the original colour. I waved my hands around it to get off as much as I could. As the dust settled to the floor, I removed its content. The photos looked like evidence, something left of someone else's life—a representation of something that doesn't exist, a lie—and my first thought was to burn them, but I didn't. I put them back on the shelf where the box had come from.

I opened the top drawer, where she'd kept her underthings. Nylons and bras and panties, worn when she was young and then put in a drawer, too precious to continue being destroyed. The drawer was packed behind new clothes of lesser value, hanging from the top of the dresser and piled in front of it. Those things were already at the dumpster and probably gone. These things, I picked through to find matching sets, coordinating outfits. I laid them out on the floor, where the couch used to be where she'd slept, then I took each set, folded them into a sheet of newspaper like tissue, and placed them in the box.

Seven sets for one week, I don't know why that seemed important.

When the box was full, I grabbed the tie from a black satin robe at the bottom of the drawer, and I tied it around the box like a ribbon. It wouldn't stay, but it wouldn't have to. The robe would be useless without it, but there was no one left to wear it. A week ago, I'd put her lipstick aside, the colour she held onto, never using, in case one day it was discontinued. I put it on before I ruined it, writing on the velvet-ish box, using half the tube on greasy, irregular letters: "Dear Edward, I miss you." The greasy font wouldn't run in the rain. I put my work runners back on and opened the door, closed it again. I carried the box down the road like I was delivering a cake to a birthday party, hands in front, holding it upright, steady. I walked the three steps up to Edward's door, set the box down on the world's saddest welcome mat, and before I left, I kissed the peephole.

The way back, my task completed, was colder than the way over. It was almost 10pm, and Brian's parents would be mad if I called this late. But I would call. They would add it to the list of things I'd done wrong, feel themselves justified in their initial impression of my inferiority, and hope that I didn't end up pregnant, even though as Catholics they couldn't advocate for anything to prevent that.

And everything their son did was forgivable.

I'd be solely responsible for his downfall.

Confirmed in the name of Saint Christopher.

Torn from the hand of God by me.

Brian picked up the phone and told me that I shouldn't have called so late. But he didn't mean it. He meant to mimic the words of his mother, spoken while the phone was still ringing, something to be passed on in a voice that might matter. "Tell her she shouldn't call so late," she would have said, the utterance delaying him picking up the line, the disturbing sound of the cordless phone extended so that she could express her disdain for its ringing without being heard.

I hear you, Connie.

I heard Brian walking away from the common area of the house, the change in reverberation as he walked down the hall, and the sound of his bedroom door closing.

"Hello," he said, to indicate we could now talk.

"Hello," I answered, and with a tone indicated this conversation would go well, that we were on good terms, that if he were closer, I'd have his clothes off.

"Hello," Brian said again, because he'd understood.

"I wish you were here."

"So do I."

"What are the chances you could be?"

"Slim to none. I promised Connor a ride in the morning."

(The brother.)

"That's really too bad."

"I know."

"Hey, I wanted to talk to you about something," I started, now that the tone was set.

"What's that?"

"Are you all right with us?" I asked him. I knew he wouldn't be but say he was, because he probably felt a little displaced, after Vincent. I knew that if I let that go too long, he might start coming up with his own reasons to feel that way, instead of just mine. I knew that if I didn't take hold of this situation right now, it could get out of control.

Not out of control, out of *my* control.

"What do you mean?" he asked.

I had my talking points prepared. How I knew that he had the artistic temperament that meant he could handle pushing boundaries. How our relationship wasn't all about sex and therefore shouldn't depend on it. How even though I assumed he would be fine with all that I had done and was about to do, I just wanted to check in, to make sure. How relationships developed over time and people change with them, that if they couldn't do that, we'd certainly be doomed. How I couldn't live if he didn't still love me, as he always had, as he would for as long as he lived.

I took the role of the weaker to assure my place as the stronger.

Brian assured me that his commitment to a non-traditional relationship wasn't shaken by its actuality.

"I just need to know," he said, taking on a paternal tone, his gifted position of power settling into his mannerisms.

"What's that?" I asked, his subject who got what she wanted.

"Are we still getting married?"

And it actually hadn't occurred to me, that Brian would still want to marry me. But the question brought me back to the time before Vincent, when it was just us, and when he needed me to say it. I forgot that there was that caveat that would make it all okay, whatever we did, to, with one another, whatever came of it. The Catholic get out of hell free card.

I said, with the utmost certainty that it was not true: "Of course."

And I realized that was his conversational goal. That whatever he had agreed to, whatever I had made him feel, it didn't matter, because I promised. I promised him that there would come some future moment when all past moments would come undone, including the ones that I'd yet to enact. It made me wonder for a second just how much he'd been getting away with, conceptually, in light of this future moment, another chance at baptism, the expectation that no matter what yet happened that it could and would be erased by yet another thing that hadn't happened. That because of this fixed point in time he envisioned for the future, there was almost no limit to what I could do now.

"Of course," I repeated.

We talked about things that had happened that day and would happen tomorrow. I told him I'd spend Friday with Bridget, that I didn't think it was a good idea for him to come. That I needed to solidify a relationship with her on my own terms.

"I think you will like her," he said, and I wondered in what aspect.

When I hung up the phone, I got a sense of it—the past I'd given up as a matter of progression. The inevitability of the destruction of what had been, and how I'd played my role in it. I missed how it was with Brian in the beginning, even while I recognized that I had worked quite intentionally to destroy it—and would continue. I thought of how if someone died, I would still miss them, even if I'd killed them. How it's possible to now lament what hasn't yet been destroyed, because it will be destroyed, and I will have a hand in it.

Change is inevitable.
Becoming rules being.
And I am the source of its movement.

20

When Bridget came over, I wanted her to feel like she was in a whole new place and time, like whatever she'd been before, she'd left it behind. Like how I felt when I left this God forsaken place. Caught up in other people's mysteries.

Like how they live.

Walking home on the gravel road from the school bus stop to my trailer, I remembered coming here for the first time. When Mom told me she was buying a place. She'd paid it off in cash from the division of assets. The mortgage came later, when it turned out there were still bills to pay and no way to get her up off the couch, not for anything, not for months.

I wondered if the same thing had happened to everyone here. If something first had to break them. But that wasn't it. Most of the people here had always been here, would always be here, were part of the environment.

I had seen where Bridget lived, and I knew she'd have no frame of reference for comprehending this place. I had at least known some squalor before here. Of course, not all of it was squalor, per se, and the old women would tear my face off if they knew I'd even thought it. Their lawns were decorated the same way they were in town, with ceramic ornaments depicting animals, lights that charged in sunlight and shone into the evening, and flowers with metal petals that turned in the wind, if it blew hard enough, if the wind hadn't forgotten us yet.

Those were the parts we focused on the first time Mom brought me here. But as we sunk further into the land mass, those pretty trailers up front fell away, and the true nature of the beast underneath revealed itself, part by part. Even at first glance, it was clear that even among the trailers, there were divisions.

The nice trailers.

The shitty ones.

How do people live like this? I'd wondered.

We'll have to go into town to do our laundry.

That doesn't work if you work. If you go to school and go to work, there's no time to sit at the laundromat for 2, 3 hours while your clothes go through a wash, dry. The money adds up. $1.75 for a washer and $2.50 for a dryer which is timed to stop after half an hour, which means everything's wet and $2.50 again. 3 hours later (if the machines aren't busy), you're back at home, hanging the things that haven't quite dried, about $15 poorer, and there's still some paper that needs writing that you said you'd do while you were there, except for the screaming child you can't avoid because you frequent the same hangouts and fuck, he doesn't want to be there either. So I gave up after a few weeks of that. Washed things in the tub when I got home from work, hung them to dry near the woodstove. It always takes the moisture out of the air anyway.

I remember my mother putting a popcorn bowl of water in my room at night, when we lived in a house. That would stop the nosebleeds from the forced air heat, she said. I remember when she saved the blood from our dinner meat to put on the bedroom door at night because she'd heard no God would kill us in our sleep if she did that.

How do people live like this?

In the trailer park, I learned to keep the blinds closed and the doors locked, or else the kids would get in and mess around. One day I came home and found a candle burning that I didn't light, and while the Joseph kids denied it, I knew it wasn't spirits.

They would have fucking told me.

The gravel beneath my feet was moving, writhing like it wasn't stone. But it felt as hard as ever, and it didn't affect my stride, and that's how I knew I didn't have to live reactive anymore.

Bridget was coming over, and I'd be in control.

She should be disoriented by the environment, and that's how she'd become amenable. When there's nothing left of our world to rely on, we look around for clues of how to behave. Therefore, I'd have to make it so her world had dissipated, including Brian, including Vincent, including everyone she'd brought to her house to celebrate her birthday. Including her parents and what kind of life they wanted for her. Including the duvet on her bed that cost more than I'd make in a week at the restaurant. People say things like, "You make enough money to have those things," but they don't understand that when I make money, it's already gone. I can't spend a week's income on a blanket. I shouldn't. *You don't want to.* Yes! For a good reason!

The devil thought vodka.

I told her to take a cab here, that there wasn't parking for visitors. She would know I was lying the moment she arrived. She would feel trapped and deceived but you know what, that's just going to mean that she'll need someone to make it all right again, and there I'll be.

Here I was.

Outside the structure, it looked like something that someone might play in. Like how rich people play at the cottage, or how some parents buy small houses for their children to put in the backyard. If there weren't so much conceptual baggage attached to the idea that it was a trailer, all of its destitution could be passed off as an element of the experience. Inside, you could almost pretend that nothing outside mattered. I put a few things in order and went back outside.

I said I'd meet her out front.

I knew she would show. She wanted me to like her as much as I wanted what I wanted from her.

Bridget paid the man $10 and immediately, I touched her hair. On one hand, I wanted to see if she'd let me do it, but on the other, my plans depended on eliminating the physical distance between us, preferably immediately. Once a precedent is established in a social interaction, it tends to carry on of its own accord, by inertia.

"Your hair is so shiny," I told her.

"I don't do anything special to it," she said. "Just wash and condition."

Her hair had never known the drying power of dish soap.

Isn't that something special?

She had a learned humility, and I knew it was because that was the recommended demeanor for a girl of her age with her prospects.

The thing about social structures is that you can depend on them.

I let my hand glide down her spine and watched her shiver.

"Come in," I told her and nudged her toward the side entrance. The front door had been locked since two months after we moved in, when Mom put a dresser in front of it. There was simply nowhere else it could go. She said it was for me, my dresser. I'd finally have somewhere to put my things away.

It wasn't a gift.

I let Bridget walk in first, and I think that made her feel like she had made her own choice in the matter, despite my being right behind her. There was a mat for us both to remove our shoes. When she was ready, I grabbed her hand and led her through the next doorway into the living area / kitchen. Everything had become clean, but the walls still existed. Wood panels that seemed to have nothing but air behind them. After Mom died, I started putting up posters. I used thumbtacks, ruining the panels, or at least that's what I thought, because I swore I could feel air coming through the holes when the thumbtacks fell out.

I had chai tea steeping on top of the woodstove, glass mugs on the table. There was a clear place where she was expected to be, and she happily went along with it. I had thought she was a little shy, but it turned out she didn't mind talking at all. While I asked questions about her life, her interests, her hobbies, what kinds of things suited her and what didn't, what she wanted, what she felt and dreamed, I could tell it made her happy that through all this I would know her.

When they say that giving personal details about yourself to a killer might make them conceive of you as a whole person and stop them from killing, they forget that out of all the killers in the world, most murdered someone they knew and loved best.

"When Brian told me about you," she eventually confided, "I didn't know what to think. He said we could be friends, but I didn't really believe him. I didn't think you could be friends with someone whose boyfriend you've kissed."

That stung, actually. Thinking of when Bridget came into the picture, what Brian and I were like back then. It was probably before Vincent had even come here. It wasn't that I was upset now, it was that I would have been upset then, had I known what had happened. I would have felt such a keen sense of loss, such a brutal and sudden awareness of how much other people considered their lives private, that even though we spent most of our time together and fucking non-stop, Brian had still found a moment to romance another girl, share what I assumed to be an innocent kiss, reassure her that it was all right, even though at the time *he wouldn't have fucking known.*

He could have ruined everything we had, if I hadn't done it as well.

"Sometimes," I told her, "a boy will make it seem like what he does... has a larger effect than it does. Do you know what I mean?" I laughed like she should.

"Like when I saw Mr. Johnson out back smoking, and he thought I was going to tell on him and begged me not to?" She giggled, like she was revealing a secret.

"Yeah, sort of. Like he definitely thought he was the main character of that interaction, right? Like he thought all that mattered was *what he did* and how you reacted to it."

"Yeah, like how did he know I wasn't also up to something?"

Honestly, you could tell by looking at her. But instead of saying that, I said, "It wouldn't have occurred to him."

"Huh," she said.

I made more tea and without asking, I poured two ounces of vodka in each of our cups.

"What is this?" she asked.

"It's what we do out here for fun, besides talk to our new friends."

"Of course I know what alcohol is, but what is this?"

"Vodka."

"I thought you weren't supposed to taste vodka."

"They lied to you."

"That makes me feel a bit better, actually."

"Are you worried about getting your drink spiked?"

"Not anymore. This is drying my mouth out."

"Yeah, sometimes they'll make you fear something you shouldn't."

"I'm starting to feel that way." And I knew she meant to agree with me. To express some commonality between us. To take up her subordinate role as my mentee.

The thing about a mentee is, they always get to learn something. It's not a thankless role at all. And I was starting to feel full of ancient wisdoms.

"Bridget, I'm sorry if Brian made you feel like you should feel bad for liking him, if you liked him. Who knows. What I need you to know now, is that I'm here. I'm here, and I do think I know better than some boy who thinks the world revolves around him. And I know these guys. So if you ever have anything you want to know, I'll do my best to tell you. All right? Don't let them think they're in charge. Or let them, but know they aren't."

Bridget didn't look very sure.

I needed her to express her own positive affirmation; make the motions and the sounds of someone who agrees. That's the only way to make it stick. I moved around the table, took both of her hands, and I stood her up in front of the fire. Her hair shone like it was made of something else, some better quality material that they told me was no different from the one I could afford. *Just better advertising*, my Mom would say, insisting that some fabric or soap or vacuum that definitely wasn't as good was, in fact, as good.

Bridget was a better quality human than I was. Better made, better cared for, and better loved. But I could make her love me. You don't have to be loveable to be loved. Some people even insist that the worse things are better.

And I had the devil, who insisted that at the backs of her perfectly moistened blue eyes, her retinas weren't attached with any better quality stitching than mine were. He made me look at her skin, soft and smooth in the fire-light but at the same time, covered in pores and capable of emitting foul odours. She was shorter than I was and from here, I saw firm curvature suspending the fabric of her shirt out enough that some of that flesh was visible, while the devil pointed to a stretch mark she couldn't escape.

The curse of having had to grow into a human form from something other, something so small that before Bridget existed proper, she'd had to inhabit someone else's body like a parasite, as we all did, that body ruined as they all are over time and by trauma.

But the fact that Bridget was human wasn't a drawback, is what the devil didn't get (or maybe he did). The point was to have something so tenuous and yet so desired, perhaps because of its fragility, and then to ensure its potential for destruction is enacted not by time, but by force.

To replace some of the things that might happen to Bridget in her life with things that I might do to her instead.

Standing and facing her in front of the fire, I asked her, "Are you with me?"

And because she knew how not to ruin a moment, she nodded instead of answering.

I took her hair in my right hand, twirled it between my fingers, then grabbed it, slowly forcing her head back. I put my left hand behind her shoulder, because as I wanted to unsteady her, I didn't want her thinking I wouldn't be there for her when she fell. As I kissed her, her hands rested on my hips, and I felt her gently pull me, wanting more.

But I wasn't going to fuck her today.

I wanted her to love me first.

That's how you really ruin someone.

21

Edward wasn't at the window when I walked by on the way to work. The curtains were drawn. Another long day at the restaurant before I could come back home, shower, and then go out with Brian and Vincent. We were supposed to watch a film that Brian had read was good. Something by Herzog or Tarkovsky or Kurosawa. We'd go to Bridget's basement. Brian would pick up Vincent early and go to the independent video store. More and more of their stock wasn't videos at all, but video-adjacent products meant to keep the doors open. Local artisans. Fresh juice.

But first I had to put in ten hours. I traded with Molly so that I could come in at opening, leave by six, when the dinner rush had received their orders and the rest was all dishes for Jackson. I felt like I was dressed in a clown costume—comfortable shoes that used to be Mom's. White Keds, because they could be washed. I could have put them in the dishwasher—if we'd had one. But I don't think Jackson would appreciate if I came back with a stack of plates and put my shoes on top.

I'd be in the kitchen most of the time, because of Molly and the chemicals. At least that would be nice. I started checking the fridges to make sure we had everything in them we'd need for breakfast and lunch. I checked the salads to make sure they were still good, and just as I had opened a Tupperware container of pasta salad and brought it up to my nose, Jackson yelled out "Behind!", there was an impact on my shoulder, and Russian dressing spilled down my front.

"What the fuck!" I yelled, as Cheryl came into the kitchen.

"Jackson, what the fuck did you do?" she asked him.

"Nothing. I said behind, and she didn't move."

"That's not how it works," I said, rubbing the dressing from my bare neck and shoulders with a tea towel.

"Maybe you should let my mom check the salads."

Then I understood. He was pissed that he'd have to stay late, because Molly was staying late. He wanted a ride somewhere or some shit.

"Put an apron on," Cheryl said.

So I did. I put an apron on over my clothes, creating a nice hot box to concentrate the spice and vinegar of the blood red dressing. Sometimes you do the best you can and still have to smell for another nine hours. I imagined all the showers I would take next year when I left here, how in between them, I wouldn't become so soiled. How each progressive day, I'd wash more and more of this place off of me, until one day it was gone. At the same time, I thought I could see my eyes receding, the whites seeming to expand as the skin around them grew dark and taut. I could tell myself it was work or the exhaustion, but I knew that it was him.

A woman I didn't know made a remark about the red stains on my shoes, whether it was blood, whether it was sanitary. I heard it whispered from across the room to another patron. I stared at her until she knew for certain I was doing it on purpose, then I pulled my lips back from my gums and clicked my teeth at her twice.

"Did you see that?" she asked her friend, who shook her head.

I made a pot of decaf for Dave, even though it was morning, who swore that now it didn't matter if it kept him up or not, it was that he liked the taste.

Then he pulled me aside and whispered, conspiratorially: "Russian dressing?"

"Yes," I confirmed.

"I could tell by the smell," he said, happy with himself for having solved the mystery on behalf of all of the citizens of the Havsumfun mobile home park.

He went on: "Listen, I need a young woman."

And I was nice, so I told him straight out: "You can't just say that anymore, Dave. You have to say for what."

He laughed.

"Christie's putting on a talent show. I've always thought I'd be a great MC."

"I bet you would be," I said, and I meant it. He had that hair that swept off to the side. He kept his face carefully tanned, and when he laughed, it sounded affected, like he was always faking it for an audience who wasn't yet there.

"I want to do a beauty pageant of women through the ages," he said.

"Uh huh."

"You'd be the young, beautiful woman. Before you, I'd have a little girl, real cutesy. Then you'd come on like Miss America, beautiful, regal. Then my buddy'll come on in his wife's dress."

"Sounds like you've got this all planned out."

"So will you do it? It's this Thursday."

"Yeah, Dave, I can do it." Maybe it was the stench of body temperature dressing, but the thought of being beautiful sounded nice. I could show all these people that I wasn't just a waitress, a server with my hair back in bad shoes.

"Oh, thank goodness," he said. "Thank goodness."

"No problem, sounds like fun."

"I'm sorry I had to ask you, but Vicky already said no," he said, turning back to his table, putting his arms out to the sides as if to express the size of his victory.

I went back to doing my job.

22

Later that night at Bridget's, Brian was going on about how most sex isn't about sex, it's about ruining someone.

We were watching Rashomon. Bridget said she thought she'd like this movie because she didn't usually watch things with subtitles, while Brian and Vincent were happy to have someone new to patronize.

"Why do you think sex would ruin someone, though?"

"Because he's Catholic."

"Fair enough."

The fact that he didn't distinguish between sex and rape was a little concerning.

"Sex is just rape that you agreed to."

"That's fucked up."

"No, it's not. Every time a woman gets fucked, it changes her DNA."

"It does not."

"It does. My Dad is a doctor."

"What if the guy is wearing a condom?"

"Then it doesn't count. He has to ejaculate in her."

"You're fucked up."

"What about the guy and his DNA?"

"Doesn't matter. He's not the one carrying children. If a woman fucks multiple men, then any child she has will have multiple fathers."

"What the fuck, Brian?"

Vincent let his tone drop off, like it wasn't a question.

"Someday you're going to have to outgrow your parents," he said.

Brian went pale. He was used to shooting his mouth off. He was used to being respected as an intellectual, especially among his peers. He never thought that anyone would ever imply he was somebody's child.

"You don't know what you're talking about," Brian muttered.

Genetics aside, he had a point. We do define people according to what's been done to them, not what they have done. That's where God had it all wrong. There wasn't a judgment at the end of your life of all the things you had done. There was a judgment of all the things done to you. Most of the reason you are the way you are has nothing to do with you. There shouldn't be commandments, I thought. Not ones that tell you what to do and what not to do. What's really important is what's done to you. Done and not done to you. God says thou shall not kill and thou shall not steal, but worse off is the person who's dead or has nothing to offer.

If God is pure activity, then being passive is the problem. For everything that's done to you, without your having done it, you're worse off than you were. For all that fucking moralizing, the gospels forgot to mention that the best of all beings is the thing that's *doing*.

To be done to is the real sin.

Brian's problem was that he thought sex was something you do to people. And fuck, maybe it is.

Vincent sat in the armchair while I was on the couch between Brian and Bridget. I crossed my arms in front of my chest and with my left hand, leaned closer to Bridget on my right. She crossed her arms too and ran her fingers across mine. I touched the side of her breast and felt the tissue contract in response.

That was something I did.

23

I AM WHAT ISN'T ALL LOST
I AM YOUR MOTHER'S DEAD HOUND
I AM EVERYTHING THAT STINKS WITH IT
HOWEVER, I'M NOT TO BE FOUND

On the way home from school Thursday, I noticed Edward's lights were off. The talent show is tonight. Is Edward coming? He'd never come down to the restaurant; he always said he'd rather save money, eat at home. But he'd come out every once in a while, if Mom asked him to. Maybe now that she was gone, he'd realize that no one was going to make him do the things he wanted to do, so he'd have to do them himself.

I never had that problem.

For me, it was more that the things I wanted to do couldn't be done, at least not by me. I wasn't born for it.

But Marilyn wasn't born for it either. She came up on her own with no one to prop her up, probably a lot of people trying to hold her down, but there was some magic about her. I like to think that people didn't have to think about whether Marilyn deserved to get where she got; they just knew. Like when you see someone somewhere they obviously don't belong, and so you try to help them find their place. Marilyn was like someone's grandma walking into a rave; the right thing to do is figure out where she's supposed to be and get her there. I think that's what happened to her, how she got into modeling, acting, production. She was meant to be loved.

If enough people could see me too, maybe I'd end up somewhere I belonged.

Not here.

SPECTACLE IS A VOLUNTARY DELUSION

The image of Marilyn dancing in a pink dress on a red stage, covered in diamonds. I didn't think the diamonds took anything away from her. I'm sure the ones in *Gentlemen Prefer Blondes* were fake, the movie and the stage production. Even fake jewelry costs, though, and more than I could pay. Fake it till you make it, but only if you can afford to.

It's not that I even wanted to act or perform or be on a stage of any sort. That wasn't the point. Performers make themselves an object for other people, all types of people, something for the worst of us to look at and deride. I remember once my cousin, talking about the singer Jewel and how while she wasn't the hottest, he'd still fuck her. That's the kind of thing people say about performers.

No, the point was to be perceived and then, ideally, swept away, somewhere else proper. Somewhere loftier, like Strindberg said. Some of us are from somewhere loftier, and that's why everything around us seems so destitute, by comparison.

I'd thought through my outfit for the talent show over the course of several days, refining the combination as best I could. I had a black strapless top that held its shape and moved like Marilyn's. If I wore the black skirt with it of the same structured material, it would look like a dress from far away. I had mother's pearls and her gloves from her third wedding. The gloves were white and went up to my elbows. I'd have to be careful not to touch anything that might sully them. The pearls were probably fake; it didn't matter. They were something to put around my neck that matched my forearms and so recalled the pattern of Marilyn's outfit at least, if not the colours.

In the bathroom, I cut my hair to my shoulders, so I could curl it up like hers. I didn't get an exact bob, but it was close enough, and styled, it gave the impression of something that it wasn't—a hairstyle that wasn't just botched or by accident. Black eyeliner, white eyeshadow, mascara, red lipstick.

No tights. I didn't have any left after what I'd given to Edward.

I walked down to the rec centre with my best coat over my costume and the idea that someone might figure out I shouldn't be here.

I should be wherever it is people like me go.

I hadn't told Brian or Bridget or Vincent about the talent show. I couldn't imagine what kind of impression they'd have of me if they saw it. Participating in the community. Putting in the effort. It might be counterproductive. I was trying to prove that I didn't belong.

At the rec centre, I told Christie I was a performer, and she told me I could sit in the front row of the auditorium until it was Dave's turn. He'd come slightly after the first break. I could feel that my hair had shifted after the walk in the wind, and there was a mist in the air I hoped hadn't ruined my eyes. I couldn't get to the bathroom to check from the front row, all the way in the back. People would see and notice me incorrectly. I should be loved, not walking to the bathroom.

I determined I'd have to check on the break. But during the break, Dave wanted to get organized. He had this child dressed up in some poufy white and green number, a tiara on her head, brown ringlets. Someone had done that to her, I thought. Someone who cared. She was first in line to walk up and down the stage. I remembered practicing a runway walk as a small child, once I discovered that there were people who were paid to model clothes. People told me I was pretty, and I believed them. At the end of the stage was a chair. The aged fellow behind me was Dave's friend, the image of mocking beauty ideals. He was also in his sixties, painted wrong, wearing a sun dress he'd probably pulled from his wife's dresser, without thinking that the good dresses would be hung, the ones appropriate to an evening event.

The music came on after the break, and then Dave started talking over it. Lined up at stage right, the little girl walked on stage as Dave invited her to come sit in the chair. He asked her some questions for a child beauty queen, the audience of about 50 aged residents cooing at her responses.

"What's your favourite colour?"

"What's your favourite school subject?"

"I like art class," she said, and it was a hit.

Looking at the audience, it was getting harder to imagine any one of them could save me. These were all just people who lived down the road, down the block, down near the front of the park where the lawns were tended. What was I thinking, coming here?

That there would be *someone*…

There isn't anyone other than who's here.

You shouldn't be here, I knew it with the force required to move an immovable object, and yet I remained in place. It's one thing to know something and another to manifest the actions required by that knowledge. What was I supposed to do, *run?*

MY OH MY WHAT LEGS YOU HAVE

Ruin Dave's presentation?

The little girl walked off stage left, and it was my turn. I walked on stage and over to Dave, who turned me back around and had me do another back and forth across the stage. Dave gave a fictional summary of my biography and accomplishments, a joke at beauty's expense. Even so, a woman in the second row whispered, "She's beautiful," to which her friend responded, "Is that the girl from the restaurant?" and the friend nodded yes and let Dave keep talking.

What the fuck was I doing here, and why hadn't the devil saved me? He should have not let me say yes to Dave; he should have stopped me from coming. He's been quiet for a bit, but he's always there. Every so often when I'm about to do something, he says no, and I find a way out of it. But the easiest way off this stage, and I knew it, was to finish the show and go home.

Dave waved me over to the chair and sat me down, rubbed his hands on my shoulders. He made a joke about how to win a beauty pageant, and the audience laughed, even the women. Older women pretend offenses against them are funny, because they know what happens when they don't pretend. They learned it over the years.

I looked at the woman who said I was beautiful. I thought she might have a way to save me, but in her eyes was only a counter expectation that I'd save her too, from another evening at home with or without a husband, but probably a small cat whose litter box didn't really have a proper place in the 500 square foot trailer. At least if none of us were saved, we'd all have the same hovels to go back to. The consistency of it was comforting.

OH MY WHAT BIG OLD SOULS TO HAVE

Across the aisle from those woman, a man turned to another man and said, "I like this show. You can see right up her skirt."

Why would the devil have me do this?

Finally, I got to leave the stage without saying a word.

The old man in drag got on and immediately hugged Dave, who continued trying to be charming and witty as I walked from stage left to the back of the auditorium, from the darkness of that room into the glowing entranceway.

Is this what Marilyn did at the end of the day? Go home after a day of people looking up her skirt?

I thought of her leaving the movie set, to go home either to no one or to some husband or other who soon wouldn't love her anymore. How it'd been that way for her since the beginning. The profound loneliness that made me love her—that she, too, had no one to tend to her, and how when she grew up, they tried to convince her that loving someone is wanting to fuck them. How it's not believable, because when they want to fuck you, they always make it sound aggressive. The tenuous grasp on relationships resulting from how everyone who loves you leaves, goes mad, or dies—if they ever loved you at all.

I shouldn't have gone out tonight. I should have stayed alone as I was meant to be.

Is that it, *you fucking demon?*

Is the lesson to stay off the subway grate at Lexington and 52nd?

Or was it that Christie was crying in the lobby of the rec centre?

"Did you hear the news about Edward?"

24

I got my coat back and started walking toward Edward's trailer. The scene was orchestrated. People in costume were going in and out. Their clothing was designed not to be penetrated by any environmental hazards. It looked expensive. My own knockoff outfit looked cheap as I stood on the road. As more people joined me, it was clear that I fit in better amongst the onlookers than the professionals who had come to deal with Edward.

There was an unmarked van in addition to the ambulance. The lights were on, but without sirens. It was like they were doing it for attention. Did they ever think that Edward maybe wouldn't want anyone to know?

That maybe that's why he sat in there for days, not telling anyone he was dead?

The lights were on inside, and someone said they'd been on all week. But the number of flies grew until they completely covered the windows, making it seem like it was dark inside.

Where did they all come from?

Inside the box?

I think they came from Edward himself. Probably came pouring out of his mouth instead of air, once he'd stopped breathing it.

Edward had hung himself with a well-known belt, the only one he had. When they told me, I couldn't imagine anything in the frame being able to hold him up long enough to get rid of him. But they explained he used a doorknob. That made more sense.

Edward escaped this place, perhaps the only way there was.

That was why I had to do the show tonight.

To figure out that there was nowhere else to go from here.

But Edward escaped.

Edward escaped by moving as far into this place as was possible.

He picked a spot inside his own trailer, took off his only belt, and just left.

I didn't have to leave.

Or better yet, I could leave from anywhere.

The point was that Edward made a choice that made sure no one could ever make a choice for him again.

He did it himself.

He got out.

He got himself out.

Edward, I don't wish you were alive to tell me more.

Before they left with Edward's corpse, the officials opened all the windows and took the screens out. They said the flies would dissipate with the smell. Once there was nothing dead left, there was no reason for them to be here. No reason for any of us not to go home.

Part Four

25

Bridget became our mutual adored.

The four of us—me, Brian, Vincent, Bridget—spent as much time together as we could. We would meet between classes and over lunch hours. I told Cheryl I could only work weekends, so that I could have my evenings free. The bills would go unpaid for a while, but according to my calculations, the money wouldn't run out before I did.

From school, we would go to my trailer or Bridget's basement. Her parents were happy she had found such a set of upstanding individuals to spend time with. Brian was a doctor's son, and I embodied the poor work ethic they thought might be a good influence someday. Vincent had an artistic air about him that would enhance her creativity.

At school, we were two couples. It was easier to explain the relationship that way. But outside of that, they knew she was mine.

In Bridget's basement, she sat in the armchair while I explained human anatomy. I pointed to areas on Brian's body that were reactive, and I demonstrated the effect of manipulating them. I explained how my and her body worked, and why it was important to achieve orgasm.

When humans orgasm, the body allows an interchange of soul to occur, changing its formal structure while its material remains.

Bridget would watch us fuck and become aroused. I explained how to touch herself to relieve the tension, but I also let her know that it wasn't the same as when someone else did it. While their hands or other body parts might not be as technically proficient, there was something to the foreign soul in them that changed the orgasm.

Bridget admired the monsters we created in the many possible arrangements of human bodies. Sometimes we would have six arms and six legs, while other times some limbs would be hidden from view—another sort of monster. She envisioned the flesh attaching where it remained in prolonged contact, a monster made by combination rather than elimination. At the end of each session, Bridget would report back on what monsters had been formed by the three of us, what she had learned and observed.

I asked her if she was ever afraid of the monsters, and she told me no, in fact, it made her sad when, at the end, the monster would break apart and turn back into the people she knew.

"There's something more to it than you all as you are," she said.

I would kiss her, dry on the mouth, and ask her, "Do you love me?"

And she would say, "Of course I do."

26

At work, nobody wanted to talk about the talent show. News about Edward had gotten around, and it felt like people were guilty for being out having fun while Edward was dead.

The suicides didn't tend to come from our end of the park.

Edward was too young for it.

It happened every so often that someone from the nice end of the park would off themselves. It was expected, and when it happened, people would act as if the person had just died, not of their own free will, because they were old enough for that. But living here a few years, you got to know that the old people had not just a little bit of despair that would follow them here, from wherever they were. Huge financial losses. Family estrangement. A general sense of helplessness in the incontrovertible fact that their time was coming to an end, and everything they had wanted to achieve, now there was no time for it. There is such a thing as being too old to accomplish something. It's basic math. The human lifespan does have a limit, and some things they had wanted to do would take time, time they didn't have.

So it was respectful, when one of them suddenly left us, to pretend they had just died.

Of natural causes.

Unless it was a really unusual case.

Melvin Whittal, for instance—he used to come by the restaurant for takeout. He didn't want to sit alone, and he didn't want to make friends to sit with either. So he would order his food and take it home with him. "I want to enjoy it without anyone bothering me," he'd say. But we heard about how he'd once had a wife who'd left him. They said he used to hit her and then one day, he hit her too hard. At some point after the blood transfusion, she decided she couldn't go back, couldn't keep being a drain on the medical system, couldn't let another blood drive happen just because she kept herself within arm's reach of a man who would take it. And when she left, the kids stopped coming to visit. Sometimes you would see him in the driveway, tinkering with something with a motor, testing it, letting the dysfunctional ones squeal through the neighbourhood, the sound the only way his loneliness could be expressed. The rest of the time he'd sit in his trailer, the TV on too loud, the pictures reflecting on the backside of the curtains. He liked Western movies.

Melvin Whittal was found in his driveway, in the backseat of his truck. Someone saw the smoke filling up the windows and the hose from the exhaust from the window. But the air wasn't what killed him, and neither did the pills undigested in his belly. Melvin died from a rifle shot to the head; the rest of it was just backup. Melvin

Whittal was fucking serious.

"I didn't think Edward would have the guts for it, honestly," I overheard someone say at table four.

When Melvin killed himself, the mess was contained to his truck and, after the cops were called, someone just drove it away. I thought that was polite.

Edward's trailer would be harder to clean up.

"Maybe he didn't really want to. Maybe he just fucked up, like a sex thing," someone said.

"No, did you see how despondent he was after...?" someone wouldn't say, referring to my mother.

"Ohhhhh, I didn't realize they were...."

"Yes, they were," a woman confirmed.

The whole table looked over at me, and I looked down at the floor. When they left, I noticed they had tipped double what they usually would. A dollar each.

That would save me.

A rumour started going around that I would be the one to distribute whatever things Edward had in there, if any of it was still good. Flies do not simply come and go; they leave a mess behind. If not their own corpses, the fluids expelled from them. Everything inside the trailer was covered in it. I didn't know when I was supposed to find the time to clean it up.

"You can have a couple of days off," Cheryl told me. But then where would the money come from?

My calculations.

I didn't like how Edward's death was going. Not at all.

I could sense a cloud of quiet everywhere I walked. For my whole shift, the sound shifted with my motion, becoming quieter the closer I became, resuming amplitude only when I'd retreated a safe distance. I could still hear everything that was going on, but it was quieter. It was a small enough space, after all. The effect was maddening, like there was a local conspiracy to encompass me in a soundless bubble, meant to isolate me from all the goings on. Some kind of agreement to cushion me in silence, but it felt aggressive. How dare they deny me ambient sound.

It amplified my thoughts.

All this time, I kept mostly to the kitchen while Molly did tables. If I was meant to be alone today, so be it. But I wouldn't be socially coerced into grieving some man my mother wouldn't fuck, poor as he was.

I stayed on until closing, and so did Cheryl and Molly. I started doing the dishes after the grills were shut off, and I noticed there weren't as many as usual. Then when I looked out on the floor, I saw why. The tables hadn't been cleared. Molly had disappeared, and so had Cheryl. I thought for a moment that they'd finally done it, forced me into solitude, destroyed the whole of humanity just to compound my loneliness. And I thought that if I were the only person left in the world, I'd want to leave this place clean. So I brought the dishes back into the kitchen, table by table. I scraped the food and napkins off them, dried bits of gravy and utensils piled between plates, making them unsteady to carry. When the dishes were done, I took the ashtrays, emptied them into the trash and washed them. I rearranged each table setup fresh for the morning: salt, pepper, napkins, ashtrays. I took the tops off the ketchup bottles and washed them, filled the bottles from the jug in the big fridge, and put them in the beverage fridge to put back on the tables in the morning.

I took a pack of cigarettes from the shelf and lit one, flicking the ashes into the sink so as not to have to go outside or dirty an ashtray. We weren't supposed to smoke in the kitchen, but now that everyone else in the universe had died, I imagined I'd be allowed.

I opened the cash register and took a tally of what was in it, the number of fives, tens and twenties. I counted the coins and opened a new roll of quarters from the stockpile on a shelf under the till, banging it in half on the counter and adding $10 to the tally.

The sound of the bathroom door opening in response scared the fuck out of me.

Then Cheryl walked out, and I almost told her I was glad she wasn't dead.

She looked around the restaurant, and she was crying.

"Thank you," she said.

"It wasn't a big deal," I told her. "Just closing."

"I know, but it is," she said.

She looked at my tally, opened the till and counted off my pay for the day. She looked at my cigarettes and asked if I'd already paid for them, and I told her I hadn't. She said don't worry about it this time, and I thanked her. Then she thought for a second whether that was good enough for what she wanted me to do, decided it wasn't, and opened the till again to get another $20.

"Listen," she said, still crying. "Molly's lost the baby."

I didn't ask, *Was it the chemicals?*

What I said was, "I'm sorry."

"I'm going to take her home now, and I need you to come in early tomorrow."

"OK," I said. "No problem."

"And I need you to stay a little later tonight. I'm so sorry," she said, crying like it was because she couldn't stand to usurp my evening.

I nodded and told her it was fine.

"What do you need me to do?" I asked. Everything here was done, and we wouldn't do inventory until tomorrow.

"I need you to clean the bathroom," she said.

Of course, I realized. Molly is still in there.

I walked around the corner from the till with Cheryl, and there she was. The bathroom door was open, and Molly was in the corner on the floor. I could see her genitals between her bare legs, bloody from the miscarriage. Of course, she wouldn't have sat on the toilet. Imagine how easy my job would have been had she. I went back out to the till and grabbed the extra set of pants from underneath, the same shelf where the coins were kept, where all sorts of things were kept that weren't right now needed but might be. Clothes, coins, bandages, alcohol, a can of burn spray.

Molly stood up, put them on and didn't look up from the floor. She was trying to find something.

"If you've dropped something, I'll get it," I told her. "You can have it back tomorrow."

I got the mop bucket out of the back closet and filled it from in the sink, using the dustpan trick to direct the water from the small tap over the side of the basin, the water condensing in the handle of the dustpan to form a stream into the bucket two feet below. Some of the blood on the floor had already dried, and the floor hadn't been cleaned for a while before that, so it was mixed with dust and hair and lint from people's pockets, a coin here and there from a well-meaning patron who wanted to test how often we actually cleaned. I picked up as many solids as I could before I wet them with the mop, and in amongst those solids, I found something tender, something fresh.

Something made of meat.

I squished the 2cm fetus between my fingers, like I was testing to see if it was ripe, as I walked back into the kitchen and found a takeout container. A small one we would use for salad dressing to go. A couple ounces with a lid. Then from under the till I took the bottle of alcohol and filled it. He didn't have much room to swim around in there, but it was just enough to get home. Like when they give you a goldfish at the fair, tied up in a plastic bag. Except I wouldn't have to wait two hours for it to die.

27

On my way home, I stopped at Edward's place.

The windows were still open from when they took him away, but there wasn't any point going in them. The key was where it always was, above the doorframe hidden in a crack behind the vinyl. He wasn't stupid. He wasn't going to buy a rock to put it in, hide it under the mat Hiding keys under mats is only for people whose homes won't be broken into anyway. They might as well leave the key in the door. But if someone might actually want to come in, you have to be a little cleverer.

Inside, besides the rot, everything was in its place. Edward was always fastidious. You'd think that if you were killing yourself, you'd take the day off dusting and let the place go for a couple of days. But people don't change just because they're going to die. I imagined him wiping down the doorknob before he looped his belt around it.

There's a difference between squalor and filth. Squalor is the unavoidable poverty evident in the person's dwelling, environment, area of town. Filth is when you let that place go, and the dust piles up on dust, combining with humidity to form a new kind of compound, something that seems permanently embedded on whatever it inhabits but isn't. Squalor is the rust on Edward's bathroom fixtures; the rust is all that's keeping the water out of the walls. Filth is the black ring of skin flakes and scum on an old man's bathtub who hasn't bent down to clean it since his wife died a decade ago. Edward lived in squalor, not filth.

The only source of filth in this trailer was Edward himself, in particular the flies that he became. I imagined the body turning into millions of flies over the course of several days. If he's thought of leaving the windows open, they would have dispersed, and nothing would have been left. He just didn't think of it, I supposed, or he was worried about getting cold. He had tried his best. The officials took him out wrapped in the discount painter's drop cloth he'd set down before he did it. You don't just give up that kind of finickiness. You could tell where the flies had been because of the black spots, like works of fecal matter pointillism around the windows and around where they'd found Edward. Like the rest of us, the flies just wanted to get out, but it turned out they had to eat. Fly corpses dotted the carpets but not as many as you might think. I wonder if Edward thought about killing so many other things along with himself. Oh well. They probably lived a good life.

I was happy that most of the fabric elements of the trailer seemed all right. The flies didn't congregate around the living room furniture, the shower curtain, or the bed. Even though the upholstery on the couch was threadbare, dust wouldn't fly out of the cushions on impact. The dishes were organized in the cupboards, and the carpets didn't change colour depending on where people walked.

I was feeling optimistic. Edward might have some things I need, I thought.

Like a vacuum.

I hadn't done our floors since Mom died. There wasn't any point when she was alive. There was no visible carpet to clean. The carpet itself was protected with a makeshift layer of stuff that took the dust on its behalf. Edward's house, besides what was left of the flies, was clean enough; it just looked like someone took every piece of furniture they'd found on the side of the road and put it together, like a diorama meant to illustrate what it might be like to be poor.

One other spot that would have to be cleaned was the bathroom garbage can. The little black dots encircled that too, and there were still flies moving inside it. I picked it up by the edge. My hands were already fucked. If I'd had gloves, I should have put them on before I came in, but I didn't think of it and so I didn't. And I knew that the best way to overcome that ick was to treat my own hands like tools, like something to be used for a purpose and then cleaned later. Because they could be cleaned. They could always be cleaned.

Outside Edward's door, where the flies could dissipate without bumping against my face or getting stuck in my hair, I shook the trash can out on the ground. There was only one thing in it, and I recognized it from my own place.

Mom's pantyhose had gotten stiffer since I'd last seen them.

I left Molly Junior in the medicine cabinet and went home to start a fire.

28

I miss my mom.

I miss how she'd forget I was a child and act like I was her friend. How her logic worked. How on my thirteenth birthday we made milkshakes for breakfast and how now that I was teenager and "teenagers drink, you know," she decided it'd be fun to make it half scotch whiskey.

How she used to bring me to parties where kids weren't allowed and act like I wasn't not supposed to be there. How one time she noticed a bowl of Swedish berries on the snack table and whispered, "Cover me," as she turned to the corner and slipped them under her shirt, pretending they were nipples. How she turned back around went on to make conversation with her friends, and when some guy would look down, she yelled, "Hey, motherfucker, eyes up here!" while I laughed in the corner, because while we were out with them, she wasn't out *with them*, she was still with me.

She used to let me smoke inside the house, even though she didn't. I just had to open the door to the woodstove and blow the smoke inside on each exhale, because "That's what chimneys are for."

I miss what she was like before she wasn't.

How every time she got married, she thought that this time someone could love her.

Mom got married more times than Marilyn, and just like her, the men were all very different, and just like her, they didn't really mean it.

I missed all the places we got to stay. Other people's houses who had left for Christmas or some other holiday, and we got to live like we lived there. I'd put on my earphones and lie on someone else's bed and pretend that's where I always got to sleep. We'd put our gifts under someone else's tree and never have to take it down. When we couldn't buy anything, we'd bake something, as long as we could still afford ingredients. The only thing worse than being the only kid not bringing a can to the food drive is getting the same can back later.

I remember one time she broke this guy's plate and how much it cost her. You couldn't buy those in a set anymore; you had to get an antique dealer to find one that would match, hope it was the same age, a premium to buy it by the piece and two hundred dollars later, how some person's idea of what was right—replacing what you broke—might cost somebody else.

Maybe if someone had given her a break, she could have lived a little longer. Maybe that's how it works after all—that people only live as long as they're allowed, and they're only allowed to live as long as someone else takes their wrongs and says it's all right.

God damn it, I wished I wasn't where I was but that was it, wasn't it?

I wish that I'd never met Vincent, and that I didn't

fuck Brian, and that we just kept going to that bookstore, looking for the next best thing.

I miss how playful he used to be, how he used to want to impress me, how he didn't think to think the worst of me, how before he ever spoke to me, he'd look at me like I was magic.

But that wasn't how it was, was it?

Everything that seems good, there's something wrong behind it.

Brian didn't want me to pick out books with.

I'd never be enough that way.

Just like she never was to them.

There's no such thing as eternity, and the next best thing isn't circular repetitions, the next best thing is you take what you can get for however long you can get it and then die.

Drive away with Melvin Whittal in the back seat of his truck.

Borrow a necklace from Edward.

If you made it to life at all.

Just look at Molly Junior.

I missed the way my body used to feel with all its helplessness. There's something about this strength that isn't right, that isn't meant for it. This corpse that up and dies at the slightest provocation wasn't meant to hold this power. There's a time when you've been too high for too long and the comedown isn't coming and that's a concern, well, isn't it, and that's kind of what this feels like too.

I know that he made me out to do this, but it doesn't mean the body suits its purpose.

I'm waiting for my heart to give out and for my brain

to dissolve in its encasement, slosh around in its membrane, until one day it's all too much and out it comes, thick blood streaming from my nose, where they used to perform lobotomies on people like my mother.

The devil's done too well this time with me; I'm going to make it.

He's on track to make sure no one's got their head on straight when I'm done.

Because the thing is that I loved her.

That's why it hurts so bad that she's gone.

And the thing is I love Brian too.

That'll hurt like hell as well.

But it's not like I'm not going to do it.

Because I love the devil more.

Because he asked me to do what I could with what I could muster.

And because I said I would.

29

WHAT DOESN'T COME IN THE NIGHT
LAYS WASTE TO THE DAY IT DOES
AND THE UNDERBELLY OF EXISTENCE
PROTRUDES THROUGH THE LIGHT OF THE SUN
RAIN COMES FROM THE SAME PLACE AS THE HEAVENS
WHERE THE DEAD MAY FAIL TO RISE
ON THE MUTINY FORMS OF MOTION
EVIL LOOKS YOU IN THE EYE
THERE IS A TIDE THAT'S TURNING
AND IT'S NOT THE ONLY ONE
THE LITTLE BARFLY SCALES THE GLASS AGAIN
AND HER BLOODFLOW NEVER RUNS

Later that week, I brought Brian, Vincent, and Bridget over to Edward's.

"Our new place," I told them.

We closed the windows, locking in what'd got in when the police had let the flies out, or most of them. Leaves and snow and trash blown in off the road or thrown in by our neighbours. I turned on the electric baseboard heat and figured the bill would come, but not for me. I showed them the spot where Edward had lain dead, explained how the belt went around the doorknob, what all of the layers of stain meant and how to clean them.

"Let's not," Vincent said.

Brian sat down on the couch, and I leaned back against him. His arm came over my shoulder and pressed me into him, the combination of warmth and pressure both assurances he was still alive. Worse than Edward becoming cold, in his last days, he had become a thing that things were done to. Maybe the reason we feel badly for corpses isn't because of the people they used to be, but because they can't do anything on their own. How frustrating that must be.

Bridget wandered from room to room, things I'd already seen. Vincent was going through Edward's belongings. He pulled some clothes from the closet, told us to pick our costumes from them. There were work clothes, plaid and denim, worn at the points of motion. I took a white dress shirt and black vest, something bought for some cousin's wedding and saved for an indefinite future that didn't come. Bridget took the jacket that went with my vest, put it on over bare flesh, did up the button for modesty, but I undid it again.

Vincent held his camera out and took our picture.

I couldn't get my eyes straight and hadn't been able to since that night after Bridget's party. One always looked like it had wandered off looking for the underworld. But no one else seemed to notice, and we admired the aesthetic of youth in a dead man's clothes. In the photo, destitution was something to be tried on, like a Halloween costume made for one night only; fake clothes for fooling around. No one lived like that for real. Not anymore, right, Edward?

Brian had a vodka bottle that we passed around, and I'd decided it was all right to smoke inside. The smoke would drive some flies away, I reasoned. Or it would poison the air a second way. On the one hand, the scents of death made our flesh feel temporary but on the other, every perception of something was a new arrogance, the affirmation of a capacity that some people just don't have.

Bridget took my cigarette and blew its smoke into the air.

"You look like Marlene Dietrich," I told her.

"Is that a good thing?" she asked.

"It's a very good thing," Vincent told her and kissed her on the forehead.

"You should stay forever, just like that," I whispered in her ear.

But the forces of nature wouldn't allow for that, would they? Time moves forward, things decay. Cigarettes go out, and eventually, Bridget in her flesh will want to get up, eat something, put something else on. All of our attempts to make a moment freeze in time have made our subordination to motion even worse. Edward didn't want to freeze time, he wanted to escape it, and that's the only reasonable desire to have. Because even if I tied Bridget down to that spot, put that cigarette in her mouth, made her breathe in and out for days, the decay would happen all the faster. The decay that's coming for us, threatening to disintegrate.

Bridget would be best preserved in all her freedom of agency or in death. One right up until the other.

Brian had the money and the deepest voice, so he called the taxi from town to bring us more vodka. By the time it got here, the driver wouldn't care enough that we weren't old enough to buy it; returning it would be much more work than taking the money. Edward had drunk whatever he had before choking himself, which made sense. He wasn't saving it for anything anymore, not like my and Bridget's suit. I wonder if he didn't put it on because he didn't want his flesh to ruin it.

I wonder at what point he became the flesh he did, or if the flesh was merely corpse, and if that was the point at which someone became not what they were. I looked around at my compatriots and marveled at how they were all just what they were, all of their own selves. Whereas I needed the devil.

The devil was what held me all together all this time.

What made the flesh parts of my body stick to bone?

He was what made my thoughts run in order and I knew, because it didn't have to be that way, because he'd shown me what that would be like, more than a few times.

For Edward, it was his soul that held his body all together and made it not food for flies, but for me, it was the devil.

Like something that had to be because I didn't have enough soul to start.

Brian and Bridget both had souls, that much was always clear.

What Vincent was, we still don't know.

Whether it was semen he put into me or something

else entirely, a substitute like how the devil stepped in for my emaciated soul.

I wonder if we were both born that way, Mom and I, just partials, or whether it was something you were supposed to grow into but couldn't, not in this place.

A lot of monsters are just things that failed to develop into what they were meant to be.

But I hadn't failed. I was more, something more than that.

A person plus a devil too.

He said that all the time about me.

More, he said, *with me*.

I went to the bathroom and tried to see him in the mirror, and there he was. The thing making sure my eyes didn't look right back at him. I pissed vodka and wondered whether its power or the devil was in charge.

Brian was the one from somewhere better. He could have been so much more than us, if only he'd known what to hate about me. It was instinctual in the rest of them. The kids at school who had known, about me, there was something there to despise. Without saying anything, they could tell, something not in the look but the aura about it, something *not all there*, a void, and they didn't want to get lost in it. But Brian saw the same thing and thought it might be a nice place to be, just be, somewhere to go where you wouldn't be bothered and warm, like a trailer someone had died in with electric heat on a corpse's account. There must be something wrong with him too.

And Bridget, what had we done to her that couldn't be undone? We sat on the floor cross-legged across from Brian on the sofa. I leaned in toward her, grabbed the sides of her coat, did the button up. That'll help to contain you, I thought, like an extra layer of containment to the flesh. That way if her soul died, and the flesh started to rot around it, at least the jacket would keep some of it in, for a longer while, some sense of order retained.

There's an order to everything and for each of us, it comes from somewhere else. Bridget and Brian had their souls, and I think Vincent did too, of a different sort. He was something between them and the devil, something else that was a conduit for the things the devil wanted done, until of course I came along. But for me it wouldn't end that well; my flesh couldn't contain that kind of soul, and it was obvious from the smells that started to emanate as soon as he was in me. Every time Vincent ejaculated into me, the rot advanced, and while the devil made it look nice from the outside, I could tell the inside wasn't meant to last. Just something to advance the rot that was already coming, already there.

Bridget's rot was barely noticeable, still in potentiality in her form. She'd hit the apex of existence that contained within itself its own destruction, but the swell of human life had just hit its crest, so that even while its downturn was contained within itself, it hadn't become the active force of her. But it only took a second to turn a life force into a death force. And right now she was beautiful, because she held herself together, the human form and all its parts, moving in tandem to enact her will. It was so nascent that she hadn't yet decided what to want but if she did, the body would obey.

I saw a shadow beneath my own flesh that, once it surfaced, meant I was done for.

There's a shadow that infects the bones and when the flesh shows signs of weakness, it extrudes centrifugally toward the body's extremities, killing everything, until at last, it hits the perceptual organs, the eyes the penultimate death before the brain, the inner darkness killing life's light. The force that holds it all together is a resistance, a pushing back against our own interiors. When at any moment an organ or its fluids attempt escape, the soul's force enacts an equal but opposite force to keep it contained, where it is, performing its function. When if that force were to relax, for just a moment, blood and bile would leak from the body's pores, the organs would become disorganized, the flesh become something free.

Maybe death is the freedom of flesh from the soul's tyranny, the end of its servitude toward my ends.

Or maybe the soul was something like the bond between us, between me and Brian, Bridget, Vincent, an elective affinity that produced something over and above its parts, formed an organism, provided the structure according to which we might all work in tandem, toward something—toward what? What were we all brought here to do, to be? What was it the four of us were meant for?

Fulfill your end, the devil said.

I had no end of the deal, is what I thought.

Not that end, fulfill your purpose, so he said.

Of course, I knew it.

But first I wanted to lay in luxury with Brian on the couch, his warmth intermingling with what I could provide, and our parts, although symmetrical, complementary. I pushed back against his body with mine while Bridget watched us from the floor. Now that she had taken up smoking, she had something to do with her hands, and a way of adding to the atmosphere of the room.

Behind me, Brian's cock pushed up against my clothing, so I reached down and undid the button on my jeans, pulled them down enough to afford him access. Vincent, who was up and about the place again, smelled what was happening and came back into the room. Brian's rubbing became frantic, trying to find friction against my body, becoming liquid as that bit of flesh eroded from whatever Vincent had put into me. I felt its moisture brimming from my pussy, staining the couch and whatever of us touched it. Vincent knelt in front of my face and got his cock out. I repositioned myself on my elbow to get a better angle, used what control I had left to tighten my mouth around it, made a vacuum inside my head that increased as he pulled back and the space was not filled with air as it should have been. I pulled him toward me by the belt loops, felt his cock cut off my airways, thought that this is what's like to not have to breathe. The freedom of it overwhelmed me and my muscles kicked back, a dying habit of life that had become purely mechanical. I pulled him back, and in the void that I'd created, felt his acid pour down my esophagus, my reactivity so reduced so as not to cough as I felt it linger, the tissue so far gone that where once I might have sat up, coughed and sputtered, tried to find more air to breathe, I instead made do with what I had, turned myself onto my front while Brian fucked me harder into the brown plaid upholstery. I felt Vincent get up onto the arm of the couch, sit down, put his knees down on my shoulders, giving Brian some resistance.

He always said it was the push back that made him come.

"I think you've got your period," Vincent whispered to me, laughing.

But it wasn't and he knew it. I hadn't gotten one since Vincent first came inside me, sealing off my uterus or burning it out, I'm not sure. Whatever blood there was on Edward's couch, it was all mine and not some potential fetus'. Brian took his dick out, masturbated until my back was warm again, and then he took his bloody hand and made a print on my right shoulder, dragged it down to the small of my back where his hand picked up extra fluid from the semen, carried on around my left buttock, trailing off toward my thigh.

I stood up to show the others.

"Beautiful," Bridget said, while Vincent took my picture.

"Just a second," I said, walking to the bathroom and back. I took my take-out container from my last shift at the restaurant from the medicine cabinet and drained the alcohol from it. The tissue had turned darker, and I knew the alcohol wouldn't preserve it for long. When I put it in my mouth, I felt a different desiccation than the vodka, dryer because of the higher content of the alcohol. I kept the fetus in my cheek and returned to Edward's living room, the site of all deaths so far.

I kissed Bridget, and when I did it, I pushed the tissue into her mouth like I was passing her a piece of gum.

She took it from me gladly and when I said swallow, she did.

She'd always been a good girl.

30

I went back to the bathroom to shower. I set my and Edward's clothes down in the safest place possible, on top of the lowered toilet seat, and turned on the taps. The water spread out from the tap for the most part, some of it never making it to the end, draining down the wall and into the cracks where the vinyl met the tub. The tap on the bath had a hole in it, so I tried to switch it to the shower as quickly as possible, to avoid the water pressure making it worse.

Not that it mattered.

I laughed at myself.

It's that death-like freedom for possessions. The point, the whole point, was not to preserve this place but to let it go, let it all go to hell, let it fucking die already. Oh god, to be the house left behind by a dead man. If possessions were polite, they'd have the decency to fuck off out of existence when whoever owned them died.

Maybe if Edward were polite, he'd have burnt the place down when he could have. Taken all of his things with it. If he could only have erased himself effectively, but no. He put that god damned sheeting down and tried to save as much as possible for whoever came along after-ward to have it.

Me?

Somewhere, someone was driving Melvin Whittal's truck.

Is Edward up in heaven watching me fuck on his couch?

I felt something in my mouth and spit it down the drain.

Thyreophora cynophila.

I'm becoming a corpse from the inside out, and Edward died and left me his towels.

I made careful not to touch the spots that might be most sensitive to jostling. I'd have to be as much of a whole person as I could be for as long as possible. But I could see my skin wasn't breathing right; it was tighten-ing. The water didn't react to it properly. The soap didn't either. I grabbed the hand towel from the wall and tossed it to myself over my shoulder so I could scrub my back. More flies came up, and I coughed. I tried to cough as hard as possible so the contractions in my throat would kill them. So they'd go straight down the drain and not fly into the other room, where my friends were.

It's polite to deal with one's own infestations.

I put on a pair of Edward's boxer briefs and my own shirt, which I'd switched out for Edward's when arrived. Something clean enough, washed in another shower in another trailer on the same street. I felt so far from home although I wasn't.

It's a nice thing, to be amongst other people's things.

Something that wouldn't have to be here tomorrow, like my own bed or fridge. I felt wealthy, like I had extra of something for once. That trailer was for living, but this one was for play. This one nobody relied on for anything, and although it kept the cold out, it didn't have to. It did it better than my own place, because of the electric heat, but it didn't have to. From here, everyone had somewhere else to go home to.

I walked back out into the living room and sat down again on the floor. From there I poured more vodka and drank it, my heart rate increasing until I could feel it. Brian and Vincent were talking about which musicians they'd like to fuck. Bridget was still smoking, waiting to see how I'd respond, but I wouldn't.

I thought of how when I died of this, the world would go on without me, just so. Not with these same people doing these same things, but other people, similar people doing similar things, ad nauseum. The mundanity of it. Everyone had their shit, and this was mine. These were the humans I'd spend my time with until I didn't, but they could have been others. How accidental it was that I'd decided Brian would make a good boyfriend, how he didn't notice anything special about Bridget when he'd brought her around at first.

How despite all that, how badly the sentiment hit that all of them would die. Whatever is particular to these particular humans—their souls, their persons, their core—whatever it was, you could sure feel its lack. The atmosphere of this trailer wasn't that it was Edward's but that it wasn't. What we were doing here in the first place—avoiding my place—avoiding what wasn't there more than what was.

The devil knew nothing well.

That indefinite what isn't that besieges us.

Bridget put her head down on my lap, and I ran my

fingers through her hair. She wrapped Edward's jacket tighter around her flesh. It wasn't getting colder, but it was getting darker, and the feeling was the same. All at once I could feel the thinness of the walls, the curtains that kept out the gaze of any passersby, the fact that they'd see lights in the window and wonder what the dead man was doing inside, awake all night. Wondering if the police had left the lights on and if it wouldn't be polite to come in and shut them off.

Fuck it.

Fuck them.

I'd meet them at the door and say it to their face.

They couldn't take this comfort from me.

I combed through Bridget's hair and delighted in the feeling as the weight of it dragged the strands across the crevices between my fingers. I thought about the disjunct between the sensitivity of bodies where they're often touched versus where they aren't. How some parts never callous over but go raw instead, and if they aren't left alone, just bleed and keep on bleeding.

Time doesn't heal wounds, respite does. You have to stop hurting something for a while if time's going to work on it.

What if it always only gets worse?

I felt a motion in my mouth and looked at Vincent.

You can't blame something for being what it is.

And I loved him just as much as Brian.

As much as Bridget maybe, but that was something else.

I killed the fly with my tongue, pushing it up against the roof of my mouth. Then when Brian wasn't looking, I spit it in his glass. Vincent saw the whole thing and waited with me for Brian to notice. Then when he did, we laughed so hard that Bridget had to sit up because of all the jostling.

This couldn't be the end to everything.

Brian said it was fine, just extra protein, but for the first time in a long time, I thought he looked really scared.

I thought what I might like to happen next and how to make it so.

"Guys," I said to them, so they'd stop talking, but to Bridget as well. "I think we should make a film."

"Oh yeah? What's it about?" Brian asked, because he wanted to judge whatever I said next with some needling critique meant at once to demolish and impress me. But not this time.

"It'll be about ruining Bridget," I said, and the concept cut short any forthcoming pessimism.

Bridget smiled at me, nodding, while the boys talked excitedly, planning their shots.

But this would be my film, I thought.

What I left to those who outlived me.

And I didn't see any of them here.

BYE, BYE BRIDGET
MY HEART BELONGS TO THE DEVIL

SCENE 1

A girl appears on screen, 16, maybe 17. Her brown hair falls limp at the sides of her face, straight and unfussy. She sits down in an old plaid armchair, coughs once for the camera.

Girl: What is that?
Narrator: What?
Girl: The smell in this chair.
Narrator: I don't know. Probably Edward's skin.
Girl: They found his skin here?
Narrator: (laughs) No, honey. It fell off him all those years he sat in it.
Girl: (smiles) Oh, all right.

The girl looks into the camera.

Narrator: Don't look at them, look at me.
Girl: All right.

The girl looks behind the camera.

Narrator: Tell them who you are.
Girl: My name is Bridget.
Narrator: Don't look at me, look at them.

Bridget looks into the camera.

Narrator: Take two.
Bridget: My name is Bridget.

Bridget looks behind the camera.

Narrator: Good girl. Now tell them who you are.

Bridget looks into the camera.

Bridget: My name is Bridget Matthews. I live in Salem. My parents are Ronnie and Mike. My friends are you, Brian and Vincent. I like math and programming, music and art.

Bridget looks behind the camera.

Narrator: Tell them who you really are.

Bridget looks into the camera.

Bridget: My name is Bridget. I came here with my friends, you, Brian and Vincent. I wanted to fit in somewhere. I've never been in a place like this before.

Narrator: What do you mean? You've been to my place.

Quiet.

Bridget: I meant a place where someone has died.

Narrator: Not that you know of.

Bridget looks behind the camera.

Narrator: My mother died in my trailer.

Bridget's face reacts; her eyes are wet.

Bridget: I'm sorry.

Narrator: Don't look at me, look at them.

Bridget looks into the camera.

Narrator: Tell them who you really are.

Bridget: My name is Bridget Matthews. I've been in two places where people have died. But now that I think of it, a lot of people would have died in the hospital, and I've been there a lot. It's just that you never see them dying, and it isn't where they lived. I guess you have to live somewhere to die in it, or it's not really yours to die in.

Narrator: Good girl. Now why were you in the hospital?

Bridget: I'm not well, and my brother.

Narrator: How are you not well? What about your brother?

Bridget looks behind the camera.

Narrator: Don't look at me, look at them.

Bridget looks into the camera.

Bridget: My name is Bridget. I have cystic fibrosis, and my brother, Mark, is dead.

Narrator: I didn't know you were sick.

Bridget: It's not bad enough yet to notice unless you're around all the time.

Narrator: Tell them.

Bridget: My name is Bridget. Sometimes it feels like I am drowning, and I'm not sure if it's me or my lungs doing it. One day I will need oxygen all the time. Sometimes it is harder for me to move, because of all the air it takes. I thought for sure I'd die before my brother, and I think my parents felt the same way. Now I'm all that's left for them, and I'm only going to live halfway through life, only half a person, half a daughter. They always wanted two children, but they lost one and the other has only half a life and has already lived half of it. They wanted two children, and they got one dead and one half dead.

Narrator: What happened to your brother?

Bridget: It was an accident.

Narrator: You say that like you did it.

Bridget: (laughs) I wasn't even there.

Narrator: Where were you?

Bridget: At home.

Narrator: You used to spend a lot of time at home.

Bridget: I guess I wasn't worth taking out until you guys.

Narrator: Until we what?

Bridget looks behind the camera.

Bridget: First Brian, then Vincent, then you. In order of appearance, not the order of importance. You know that you're the world to me. I told you. I meant that before you, the world was something else for me, the things in it all borrowed. Someone else's things that I was using for a while.

Narrator: Tell them.

Bridget looks into the camera.

Bridget: My brother died last winter. He was my fraternal twin, but he didn't have my disease. They shut down the intersection downtown. They measured how far his blood marked the snow. They said that they could figure out how fast the car was going from that. I don't think they ever did. Just someone's bright idea about someone else's death. They didn't figure out what kind of car it was or where it went or where it came from. They told us if they did, it wouldn't bring him back. They kept the intersection closed for three hours, just enough time for everyone in town to get up, get in their cars, and see the police down there, doing something. Doing their jobs. Like it wouldn't count if no one was up to see it. What I remember is how much it wasn't about him. While one of them took the tape down, another one walked along, kicking grey snow over the blood spatter. I was standing across the street when they let the cars start to go by. She said to the other one, "No one should have to see that." When they left, I took a handful of the snow and made a ball. I took it home and left it on the front stoop. I was sad Mark couldn't come inside, but he would have melted. When spring came, it melted, obviously. I went back downtown to try to see if his blood came back as the layers of snow on top dripped off into the gutters. But he's gone.

Narrator: You believe he's really gone?

Bridget: They tell me that he's living on, in heaven or our hearts, but I think if that were true that I would feel something.

Narrator: And you don't.

Bridget: I felt like I was the only one who couldn't.

Narrator: And then?

Bridget: You told me what happens to people who die, the lies we tell people about them, the ways that we pretend. It was never fair of them to think that he would live forever and that I wouldn't. It's not fair of them now to expect me to live on as long as I possibly could. And most of all, it's not their decision.

Narrator: People are dying all the time.

Bridget: Some of them more than others.

Narrator: Who decides when people die?

Bridget: Sometimes they do, sometimes someone else.

Narrator: Are you going to let them decide for you?

Bridget looks behind the camera.

Bridget: No, I won't.

Narrator: Don't look at me, look at them.

Bridget looks into the camera.

Bridget: My name is Bridget Matthews. I'm going to die like everyone else. I'm not going to kill myself. Killing someone doesn't take their death from them. I'm not going to kill myself, but I will die when I want to. I am choosing to die but not kill myself. Whatever happens, I don't know if I'll want it, but I know I want to die.

Narrator: You don't think that you'll live on? See Mark again?

Bridget looks behind the camera.

Bridget: I'm hoping that I don't.

Narrator: Good girl.

Bridget is walking ahead of the camera, which follows her path into the dark woods. On Bridget's right, a boy just taller than she is, dark hair, broad in the shoulders but still slight. His jaw is prominent. He has a liquor bottle in his right hand—clear liquid. His left hand swings, not freely, awkward until it moves over to the right hand, screws the cap off the bottle and vacates the space, the right hand offering the bottle to Bridget. Bridget takes the bottle and drinks, like she's thirsty from the walk. She hands the bottle back, the boy takes it, and it goes back into his right hand, away from her.

Narrator: Look at them, Vincent.
Vincent: The way he keeps his left hand.
Narrator: In case she wants to hold it.
Vincent: She knows.

Bridget lets the boy's hand touch hers and then evades its grasp.

Narrator: (laughs)

Bridget looks over her right shoulder and smiles, the angle distorted such that her companion isn't able to perceive the devil in her grin.

Vincent: Shhhhhhhhh (laughs)
Narrator turns the camera around so her face is visible, puts a finger to her mouth, pretends it is stopping her from laughing.

A pause.

Three figures appear when the camera returns, seated in a clearing. Bridget and Brian are gathering sticks, while Vincent pulls scraps of paper from his pockets, bunches them together. The mass is collected within a circle of rocks. The camera focuses on the growth of the burn pile. Voices are heard.

Vincent: Bring everything. If it isn't dry, it'll dry by the fire.
Brian: There isn't much out here.
Bridget (quietly): There is, if you look for it.
Vincent: Uh oh.

Slender pale hands gracefully arrange.

Vincent: Do the honour?

The narrator hands the camera to Vincent, who points it at her face. In the dark, her features meld together, the sockets of her eyes drawing downward, one with a widening lack, culminating in a screaming void, no discernible depth to the throat it reveals. Light flashes from her hand, illuminating away the perception, a pretty blonde girl all that time.

The fire expands the camera's field and colours its objects more lifelike.

Brian sets his contributions down next to the fire, puts his jacket on the ground and invites Bridget to sit with him.

The jacket forces their proximity, the threat of touching the ground on either side excuse enough to sit close.

They speak quietly, hoping that the two on the other side of the fire won't hear, or assuming that they would. The camera adjusts to low volume.

Bridget: Why would you even want to? When you have her?

Bridget gestures to the narrator.

Brian: All relationships end, and it's unnatural to force them. Knowing particular people at particular points in our life develops us, makes us fuller. Attachments hold us back.

Bridget: Don't you think people can change together?

Brian: Yes, but it's not the same. Why would you force something to live that's meant to die?

Bridget: I don't know. I always assumed that happily ever after meant forever.

Brian: It's a conspiracy against change. Look at her.

Bridget looks across the fire, almost into the lens.

Bridget: She's beautiful.

Brian: Yes, and I would never ruin that.

Bridget: What were you doing, when you came to my birthday party? Is this what you wanted?

Vincent: (breaking the illusion that the voices aren't heard on this side) The funny thing about best laid plans is that people don't even make them. They carry on as their whims decide, not knowing why they do the things they do, pretending afterward there was a point to it all, but it's like finding patterns in the stars. The plan isn't fucking there!

(General laughter)

Bridget: You don't think there's a point to it?

Vincent: There is a point to which all of this leads, but it wasn't meant by anyone.

Brian: The grand design!

Vincent: The grand design, yes, the grand designer, no! This was all meant to happen, yes, but for what end? Nothing! For whose purpose? No one's!

Vincent stands and takes the vodka bottle from Brian.

Narrator: Don't waste that on the fire.

Vincent: Doll, I wouldn't dream of it.

Vincent kisses the narrator like Marilyn Monroe kisses Tony Curtis in *Some Like it Hot*, leaning over her, one hand on each side of her face.

Narrator: I promise, my dear, it's all for nothing.

Vincent: (raising the bottle) To nothing!

Bridget: (taking the bottle from Vincent) For nothing!

Bridget takes a drink. Brian takes Bridget's other hand.

Brian: I wish we could go back to that party now.

Narrator: It was a lame party.

Vincent: Half of the celebrants weren't even there.

Brian: Was that a dead brother joke?

Bridget: It's true, Mark wasn't there, and we didn't invite his friends.

Narrator: A lame excuse for everything. *Sorry, I can't, I'm dead.*

Bridget: (laughs) It's like that, though. It feels like every day is a new day that he doesn't show up somewhere I want him to be.

Vincent: The same reason every time.

Narrator: Doesn't it get old?

Bridget: (laughs) You know, it does? How many times do you have to remember that someone is dead before you stop expecting them to be there? (Laughs.) How many times? How many days? You know my Mom still sets the dinner table for four?

Vincent: And what do you do with the leftovers?

Narrator: (laughs) Think of how much money you could save, by remembering Mark is dead?

Vincent: Yes, how do you make it stick? We have the family vacation to worry about.

Bridget: (laughs) I don't know. I don't know.

Brian: I don't think this is funny.

Narrator: But you don't get to decide.

Vincent: Yes, who does get to decide?

Brian: I didn't say I get to decide, but I do get to think.

Narrator: Think away.

The laughter stops. The bottle circles around the fire. Bridget picks up leave and bits of bark from next to the flames and adds them in. Brian's eyes shine against the light. He turns, puts a hand to his face, turns back.

Brian: If I could go back to that party now, I wouldn't have left. I would have stayed until the end, helped you clean up, inspected it all for damage. I'd have helped with the dishes and the trash, and taking down the streamers, talking so it wouldn't be so sad to see them go. I'd have told you it's all right to live without Mark being there, that just because you were alone, didn't mean anything had ended. There's always something new to live for, Bridget, always something. It's only nothing if you compare it to the vastness of it all. But every day there's something, a little spark of something, if you look or if you don't.

Brian looked into the fire, tears streaming down his cheeks.

Bridget finishes the bottle, breaks it on the rocks, drops the neck into the flames.

Bridget: (laughs) That would be silly. Someone comes and does that in the morning.

(General laughter)

Bridget puts her hand on Brian's.

Scene 3

Vincent: Once you go out for a while and come back in, you can really smell the death in here.

The camera shows moving images of shoes and feet. The dance is uncoordinated. No rhythm is established. The frame focuses on a striped indoor rug, spotted with chunks of snow and mud. Voices get quieter as they move farther from the microphone. The narrator is the last to advance. Someone turns a light on in the living room. We can see the chair where Bridget was sitting in Scene 1. The narrator sits in the chair and points the camera at the other three figures, lined up on the couch. Vincent is the farthest from the camera, Brian in the middle, and Bridget is closest. Brian and Vincent look down or around the room. Bridget looks behind the camera.

Narrator: It's going to be OK.

She puts the camera down and goes to Bridget. She puts her right hand, palm first under Bridget's chin and pulls Bridget's face toward hers. She puts her tongue in Bridget's mouth. Bridget takes a moment to respond, and when she does, moves quickly, as if tasting something new, an offer that might at any moment be rescinded. The narrator puts her left hand on Bridget's chest, pushing her back. Her right thumb wipes saliva from Bridget's lips.

Narrator: I want you to be with Brian now.

Bridget nods.

Vincent stands up from the sofa and stands nearby, smoking. The narrator squats in front of Brian, takes his left hand in her right and his right hand in her left and looks up into his face. She stands, holding his hands, the cross transferring from her arms to his as she rises, leaning backward. She coaxes him to stand and move away from the middle seat so Bridget can lay down. Bridget leans her head against the far arm of the sofa, where Vincent used to be. The narrator glides above her, kisses her on the forehead, and undoes the buttons of her shirt. Bridget is wearing a black wired bra, unpadded, the shape of her nipples visible through the opaque fabric.

Bridget puts her head back and closes her eyes. The narrator unbuttons her jeans, pulls the zipper down, black cotton panties with a stretch lace band. As she pulls on the waistband, it's revealed that the panties have no cheeks. The narrator puts her finger in the top of Bridget's thong, traces it down as far as she can reach, pulls, and lets it go.

Bridget: (laughing) Hey!

Narrator: Hey what?

The narrator kisses Bridget on the mouth; the tension is broken.

Brian is smoking Vincent's cigarette. The narrator stands up, takes his hand, and puts it on Bridget's stomach.

Narrator: I bless this union.

(General laughter.)

Bridget moves Brian's hand down toward her panties. He kneels next to her, one hand in her hair, the other fiddling with the elastic lace. The narrator moves off screen with Vincent. Smoke blows into the frame from the top left corner.

Brian: Can I kiss you?

Bridget nods her head.

Brian kisses Bridget. Her head moves side to side, pressed into the sofa as far as possible.

Bridget: You're so wet.

Brian: I'm sorry.

Bridget: Kiss me again.

Brian kisses her face, lips closed, worshipping her form. His left hand caresses her hair while his right hand massages her clitoris. His fingers breach her panties through the side.

Brian: Now you're so wet.

Bridget: I'm not sorry.

Bridget pushes at the sides of the lace but she can't raise her knees high enough to remove the panties herself with Brian's body in the way. Brian takes the task from her and bunches up the underwear, putting them in his pocket. He puts his face between her legs.

Vincent's face appears on screen.

Vincent: BORING!

Narrator's voice: Shhh.

The narrator appears from left, approaches Bridget from above her head, sits on the ground and smokes. She whispers in Bridget's ear while looking down at Brian. Brian is on top of Bridget now. He kisses her mouth, and she shrieks.

(General laughter.)

Brian undoes the fly of his jeans and nudges them down a little. He holds his cock in his hand and rubs it along Bridget's labia, circling the drain.

Bridget: Fucking do it already!

Bridget shrieks again as Brian lets go of his cock and rams it inside her, stopping to let her get used to the feeling. He puts his arms down on either side of her and waits for her to stop moving. The narrator is whispering to Bridget. Brian is fucking her with increasing speed. Vincent blows smoke in front of the lens.

Vincent: Hold on.

Brian stops. Vincent gets up on the other arm of the sofa, behind Brian. He sits on the arm of it, smoking. Brian starts fucking Bridget again. Vincent reaches between Brian's legs and when he pulls his hand back, it's covered in blood and fluids. Vincent pulls on Brian's pants until his full ass is visible to camera. Vincent reaches down again to Bridget's cunt, pulls out more fluid, rubs it on Brian, rubs it on himself, pulls his cock from out of nowhere and pins Brian down.

Brian stops, afraid to upset his delicate position. Vincent grabs his right arm from the sofa, causing him to fall on top of Bridget. Brian's face presses against Bridget's collarbone, rocking against her as Vincent thrusts into him. Vincent becomes the source of all motion, Brian the instrument he's using to fuck Bridget. Vincent's right hand holds both of Brian's behind his back, while his left hand steadies Brian's shoulder providing a counterforce.

The narrator disappears from screen. Smoke is visible from the right side of the frame, drifting in from the kitchen. She returns with a black-handled chef's knife. Brian's body tenses. The narrator sits down on the floor next to Bridget, whispers something in her ear.

Bridget looks to the camera and nods.

The narrator picks up the knife from the table, moves behind Bridget's head against the armrest.

Brian: What are you doi—

Vincent moves his hand from Brian's shoulder to his mouth. Brian struggles, but Vincent is stronger. The narrator moves her right hand to the left side of Bridget's throat for leverage, digs the blade into her flesh and drags it. Blood spills. The camera knows that Bridget is a thing. Her motion secondary to the figures in action. Perception refocuses on the living.

Vincent puts his arm in Brian's mouth while Brian screams. Tears stream down his face. Every time he tries to bite, Vincent fucks him harder, knocks him off balance. Brian tries to move his hips back, but he can't, his cock stuck in Bridget's corpse.

The narrator puts out her cigarette, grabs Bridget's hair. She disappears off screen to the right, reappears with the cleaver. Brian sounds like he's saying "Oh god oh god oh god" but the words are muffled by Vincent's sleeve. The narrator's back moves in front of Bridget, her arm swings up and down. The cleaver drops to her right side on the floor and when she stands, Bridget's head is gone. The narrator walks to the camera, one hand behind her back. When she's close enough, Bridget's face appears, eyes open, mouth open. The narrator puts two fingers on Bridget's lower lip and pulls it down.

Narrator: (growling) *Pretty pretty.*

Vincent laughs while Brian screams. The narrator brings the head back to the sofa and sets it up on the armrest above Bridget's neck and shoulders. Bridget's neck is crushed against the armrest by Vincent's force. The sofa is stained. The narrator crouches behind the head, petting its hair and holding its ears.

Narrator: Shhhh. Shhhh. It'll all be over soon.

Brian: (screams) Let me go!

Vincent: Finish first.

Brian: (screams) I can't!

Vincent: Yes, you can.

Narrator: Come on, Brian.

Vincent: Come on, Brian.

Narrator: Brian. Brian.

Vincent: Brian. Brian.

Brian: OH GOD!

Narrator: (pets the head) I thought you liked our Bridget.

Vincent: You told me that you loved her.

Narrator: You used to love her face.

Vincent: It wasn't that long ago...

Narrator: Oh no, did something happen between you two?

Vincent: I could have sworn it was love!

Narrator: I thought it was for good this time!

Vincent: Nothing lasts forever, though.

Narrator: Plenty of boys would kill to be in your situation.

Vincent: Fuck her! Fuck her all to hell!

Brian: Oh! God!

Brian's face contracts, the tears squeezed from his closed eyes. His body tenses, and then releases. Vincent pulls out. Brian cries into Bridget's stomach while Vincent finishes too.

Narrator: Don't be sad.

Brian: Oh god oh god oh god.

Narrator: (moving Bridget's mouth) It's what she would have wanted.

(Vincent and Narrator laughing.)

SCENE 4

Bridget's body is lying flat, her right side against the base-board.

Her belly is swollen.

Her head isn't anywhere.

Flies.

Scene 5

Male genitals in profile occupy the left and right sides of the screen, facing one another. The right are higher up. The left are bloodier. Red is more visible on the flesh than in the darker, matted hair.

Brian: Who are you?

(Laughter.)

Brian: WHO ARE YOU?

(Laughter.)

The subject on the right is ejected from screen, his penis dangling a moment in the air from inertia before it follows its body away.

WHO ARE YOU?
(Laughter.)

WHO ARE YOU?
(Laughter.)

WHO ARE YOU?
(Laughter.)

WHO ARE YOU?
(Laughter.)

WHO ARE YOU?
(Laughter.)

WHO ARE YOU?
(Laughter.)

WHO ARE YOU?
(Laughter.)

WHO ARE YOU?
(Laughter.)

Scene 6

Brian is crying.

Vincent:

I am the transcendental that counteracts the transcendent. The disorder of the matter. For every scene, there is an unseen. You'll never prove that it exists. Negations underlie what is as well as isn't. I'm every not there is. Invisible and effective. There's no light bright enough to shine on me. Silence when you can hear it. The fear that comes at night. The emptiness of your thoughts when once they stop and start again. The swarming milieu of in betweens and reckless motions in the void. People take their lives to prove that they can feel me, the wetness on the bottoms of your feet when the ground is dry. Syphoning the air from your lungs. The bile from your liver. When cellular structures waste away, it's because I've been there. I am what's holding you back from immortality, the death ingrained in birth, the end point of every line. Over in the sense of finished, not as in above.

Have you really not considered that in every case so far, nothing gets to live, and wondered why?

Brian: I want to go home.

Vincent: I'm the other side of the story, the one in which she dies.

And it happens every time.

Every single fucking time.

You don't want to go home. You just want it to be over.

Vincent pulls Brian's body over to the baseboard where Bridget's body lies. He hoists Brian's torso against the wall, his head dangling but not severed. Vincent pulls on Bridget's shoulders until she is upright, leans her against Brian. Bridget's belly is swollen. Vincent positions the bodies in the manner of the holy family.

(Bridget's head in the role of baby Jesus.)

SCENE 8

The camera is set to time lapse.

It frames the corpses in landscape.

Three-second shots.

After six shots, the frame darkens.

Two more shots. A ceiling light is turned on.

Six shots until the sunlight returns.

The ceiling light is always on.

One voice or another intones phrases unrelated to the scene.

better worth saving than ten thousand eyes generation, of which the sea is an image despise merely human delight returned from fire and every thing dreadful pursues a tendency to the middle nor is it proper to sacrifice as it were viatica imbecility of the body dilacerate these by opposition such as the heart and the liver also not to receive the fish in a causal and celestial manner beautiful descent from highest to lowest the erroneous and the boundless possess a demiurgic or fabricative power are by no means the essence of fire

After six minutes, it is evident that Brian's body is putrefying, while Bridget's body is not.

Bridget's body is growing in its centre.

Something crawls within her flesh.

Vincent appears in frame, sits beside her, holds her hand, breathes to rhythm.

(Laughter.)

After twelve minutes, Bridget's body opens from the middle. Something comes out.

What is left of the body instantly rots.

Something is there.

Something is gone.

Something is there.

Vincent appears, lays his head on Bridget's putrid lap.

Three seconds later, something is there.

Three seconds later, Vincent is eviscerated. He is red on the inside and now all around. Red, liquid, hollow.

Three seconds later, Vincent is gone.

Scene 9

A right-angle triangle converges on the right side of the screen, dissipating on the left. On its opposite side, light shines through a crack from outside. On the adjacent side, worn weather stripping is lined with condensation, frozen in drips. There's rustling, followed by footsteps, followed by movement. Everything streaks of grey and brown until the gaze levels, becomes manageable. Sound of a door opening.

Narrator: We have to be quiet.

Shhhhhhhh... shhh... shhhhhhh...

(Laughter.)

Scene 10/31?

The camera turns left through the door, walks down three steps onto a gravel driveway. The outside of a trailer, beige-yellow vertical siding, paint chipping off around the screws. Someone went too hard with the power washer. It wasn't a difficult job, nor did it pay well. One of the odd jobs Adam did whenever he was back in the park. His Mom let him come every time, and her friends let him take what he could off their porches. The longer he did bits of work around the place, the longer they'd put up with him. Factor it into the cost. Tell Dorothy they didn't mind.

There's no shame in it.

Most thefts happen during the day while people are out, but they don't go out here. There's no workday schedule where wives wave their husbands goodbye from the driveway, husbands carrying their aluminum lunchboxes with them to the cars, tiny houses when you think about it.

Tiny houses for dead flesh.

Cooked corpses on rye.

Same principle.

The perspective turns left at the end of the driveway onto the gravel roadway. Fourth street is what it would say at the end. The name of it wasn't as festive as the park. "Havsumfun" vs. "Fourth Street." Maybe they couldn't keep the festivity up once they got in. Maybe it only seemed like fun from the outside. Maybe once they got inside, it was all they could do to count to four, and maybe they weren't counting up but down, counting down to when they got to leave again, go home, go back to their real houses that don't clatter in the wind when the storms come, like a special effect for thunder that you live in.

The camera glances in each window as it goes by. Most of the curtains are drawn. There are only five houses from here to there. Such a long way to have gone. A long time to have been missing. Maybe there'd be signs of life at home when she got there. Someone taken up residence, finally come to reclaim the metal box, sold at auction after the mortgage wasn't paid.

But things don't happen that quickly, do they?

The box takes a lot longer to rot than the human in it, even the cheap ones.

The last place on the block is dark and cold and mine and I go back in it after what's probably a week away.

No one's been in it for a while.

I wish you could feel how cold it is inside.

Not many people get to experience things this way, all of it frozen where it shouldn't be. It's a habit that we have to always think of inside things as warm, but they don't have to be. Like when you leave your gloves outside and have to lay them on the woodstove a while to heat up before you can put them on, except instead of gloves it's everything and there's nothing to touch that isn't frozen.

I put a fire together in the stove.

Even once it starts, it'll take a long while for the air to warm, and then everything in it. I pictured the heat conducting from one place to another, what kind of resistance it would meet, the front of everything warming while the back of it's belligerent, still frigid. I'd need more wood for that, but it's outside in the cold, and if I stayed within two feet of the stove or so, I wasn't.

I'd better get out before I got used to it.

I brought all sorts of wood inside, counted my paper. Cereal boxes and egg cartons from the restaurant. Potato bags would do in a pinch, but I worried about the threads and the little plastic windows and what that'd do to the creosote.

Red Bird matches bought in bulk before she died. They say you can strike them anywhere, but that's only the ones with the white tip on top of the red one, and even then, it's best to do it on the box. The trouble isn't whether the match'll light or not but what it'll do to whatever you strike it on. Leave a mark from the red part or a scorch after it's lit. That and you can waste a lot of matches trying to find something it'll strike on that's not the box.

Mom said that smell was sulfur, but I don't think it is.

In the bathroom, the water was frozen in the toilet. We used to leave the water running a little in winter, keep the pipes from freezing. I guess I didn't do that.

And you have to keep its insides warm enough.

People worry about strangers when they should be worried about the people they know. Like Adam and like me. They worry that the place'll get broken into while they're gone but not that someone they know will walk right in and have at them. They worry downtown and they worry at home, they worry when they're in and when they're out, they worry when they're here and when they're far, far away. They worry about their loved ones, and they worry about themselves and what their loved ones will do without them.

I'm worried that I won't be able to get them all before they stop me.

I'll start a fire for everyone, keep them warm inside.

I wish that I had bottles with a smaller neck, but I don't. I've got mason jars and tea towels and once I realized that any old scrap of fabric can be used but preferably the natural fibers, I figured I was set. There was gasoline in the shed that I wouldn't use for fires if it weren't a special occasion for them.

I thought of Betty Boop in the old cartoons, dressed like Marilyn Monroe except I didn't like her hair. The bouncing way everyone moved, and I couldn't remember quite clearly enough but I can picture this cartoon paperboy, moving from drive to drive on a bicycle, throwing papers everywhere they shouldn't be.

I'd have to aim better for the windows.

I'd have to stop each time and light the match.

That was his problem, not stopping for the moment it takes to throw straight. Otherwise, the velocity of the bicycle adds to the velocity of the throw, and you end up in a hypotenuse situation where you don't know where the thing'll end up once it's going.

Let them know that once and for all, I give in.

There's nothing they did wrong except be here this way, and the same for me.

At each trailer, I stopped, pulled a jar out of my grocery bag (no use wrecking the nice bags), found a window that I liked, lit the gasoline-soaked fabric and threw. I was always good at throwing. Peasant stock, my teacher told me. Meant to plow the fields. One of the things I wasn't supposed to be good at, one of those things that tipped them off to who I was and where I'd come from. Where I'd never go.

The sound of shattering glass followed by a bright light inside, like when a TV screen goes white and you weren't expecting it.

I walk ten feet down the road and do it again.

Every time I do, my bag gets lighter.

Makes the walk a little easier.

Every few seconds now, things get a little better.

Better passes for good when that's what you've got.

I'll tell them that the devil made me do it.

And that they couldn't kill me if they tried.

ACKNOWLEDGEMENTS

Thanks to Ben DeVos at Apocalypse Party and Mike Corrao for his design skills. Scene 8 includes fragments of quotations from the Additional Notes to *Iamblichus' Life of Pythagoras, or Pythagoric Life. Accompanied by Fragments of the Ethical Writings of Certain Pythagoreans in the Doric Dialect; and a Collection of Pythagoric Sentences from Stobaeus and Others, which are omitted by Gale in his Oposcula Mythologica, and have not been noticed by any editor*, translated from the Greek by Thomas Taylor.